Divided V

– for y

Steve Bowkett

Cover and Illustrations by
Tony Hitchman

Based on the novel by Gareth Mottram

Published by The Red Button Press

Elsenham, Bishops Stortford, Hertfordshire, CM22 6EN

ISBN: 9798568295761

Copyright © 2020 Steve Bowkett

Red Button Press

Chapter 1: Take a Hit.

Will Foundling stood by the well, an empty wooden bucket in each hand. Something had made him forget his errand. He frowned, puzzled for a moment. Then a strange thought flashed through his mind like a spark.

There is magic in the air!

He looked about himself, feeling confused. It was not just the beauty of the evening sky – deep blue brushed with high clouds – or the sweet smell of woodsmoke. It was not only the gentle touch of the wind or the whisperings it made in the trees nearby. Something more than that. It was as though, now for the first time in his life, he could sense the presence of the gods. People had told him before that this was an enchanted world, and that had often made him think that adults sometimes had sillier ideas than children.

"But here, now, something…"

The sound of sly footsteps coming closer startled Will out of his daydream. He spun round, stumbling back to avoid Bragg's swinging punch. His head missed the wall by a hand's width. The older, bigger boy gave a sneering laugh.

"The fool talks to himself. Ha, because no one else will talk to him!"

So saying, Bragg jabbed at Will once, twice. Will dodged these lunges but not the third blow that Bragg launched with his left hand. Lights exploded in Will's eyes and he crashed to the ground, his head ringing.

Vaguely he was aware of two other people now standing close to Bragg – they would be Bragg's girlfriend Wilda and his best friend Randolf: thuggish bullies like Bragg himself.

Anger rather than fear swirled up through Will's chest. He thought about moving, getting himself out of this trouble. But Bragg loomed over him, his thick legs propped either side of Will's hips. Will caught a whiff of stale sweat from the boy's grimy body.

"You are a weakling," Bragg said. "*Naht* – a nothing. You will never be big and strong enough to join our Shield Wall. As if I would let that happen anyway!"

Bragg straightened and stepped to one side, aiming to deliver a damaging kick to Will's ribs. Will guessed the boy's move. He twisted away, grabbed the handle of one of the buckets and smashed it into Bragg's leg as he raised the other to deliver the kick. It gave Will great pleasure to see the apprentice to the king's champion topple backwards and hit the ground with a thud.

But now of course there will be more trouble!

Will scrambled up, his head spinning. He leaned against the stonework of the well to steady himself.

Bragg got heavily to his feet, rubbing his injured leg. Randolf and Wilda stepped up beside him like guard dogs protecting their master.

"So is that how you learned to fight – you snivelling coward."

Will just managed to stop himself smiling. Here was Bragg, bigger, older, with two lapdogs to help him calling Will a coward! But he said nothing, knowing that would only make things worse. His head was clearing a little now, though his cheekbone throbbed where Bragg's blow had caught him. He let his body relax and his thoughts settle. If Bragg was going to stir up more trouble he wanted to be prepared, as best he could be.

But it was Wilda who stepped forward. She began tying back her long yellow hair. Her eyes, blue and flashing contempt, fixed on Will.

"Let me deal with him," she growled. "You should not lower yourself to fight with the worm."

Will shrugged lightly, hating again the arrogance of these people. The insults did not bother him, since they had been flung at him so often before (though he knew Bragg and his friends would be enraged if *he* used them). And he didn't want to fight with Wilda but realised he would have to if she made the first move. He did not fancy his chances of victory. Like Bragg, Wilda was solidly built and, at seventeen winters, three years older than Will.

The girl spat into her palms and raised her fists. The last of the low sunlight shone on her face, turning her skin red to match her rage.

"Will Foundling – Cook needs that water now!"

A new voice rang out, high and clear, from the longhouse fifty strides from where the group was standing.

"Do I have to tell him that the king is to be kept waiting while you play silly games with these two dullheads and some giant of a lady?"

Now Will could not help but smile at Bridget's sarcastic comment. She strode up beside him, matching Wilda's hot tempered glare with one of her own. Like Will, Bridget stood outside the common circles of friends in the capital. She did not seem to mind. And by keeping herself to herself, she made others cautious. Will knew that she was an apprentice scribe and a battle runner, though serving as a kitchen maid during this journey north to the Romani Wall. Also, she seemed to know everything about everyone in the settlement. But her lack of fear now perhaps meant that she had other skills that

Bragg and his friends sensed but did not want to test.

Or maybe, thought Will, she is just being very stupid.

Will had not taken his eyes off Wilda as Bridget spoke: Wilda was dangerous, especially in a fury. And yet she did not attack. She seemed a little wary and her face now looked sullen rather than enraged.

Randolf's reason for keeping back was different. He turned to one side and spat at the earth.

"This one –" He jabbed a finger at Bridget, "if she's feeling spiteful can see to it that no venison leftovers go to the apprentice Shields. Then they'll take it out on us."

"I am bigger than spite," Bridget said. Her tone was hard and level. "And I am bigger than the cowardice that sets three against one." She cocked her head to look at Will and gave him a smirk before staring back at the others. "But three against two would be a fair fight."

Will groaned inwardly at her bravado.

"Why don't we find out...?" Bragg's words sounded like stones grinding together. He took a step forward. Will put up his fists and sighed at the sinking feeling in his stomach. He had been brought up on back-street brawls and had already had three years' military training. But Bragg, built like a stockade post and whose blood was up, would be a hard opponent to beat.

Then, surprising them all, Bridget took a step forward and held up her hand.

"Of course, your master is already cursing your name at having to pour his own mead. I can tell him you're too busy if you like."

That stopped Bragg in his tracks and sudden fear swept over his face.

"Thunor's hammer. He'll half kill me if I don't get back." He dropped his fists but strode up to Will and jabbed him in the chest with a stiffened finger. "The little kitchen wench has saved your ugly face this time. But there will be other times."

He made to barge Will aside but Will turned and sidestepped away. Randolf and Wilda followed a pace behind, each giving Will and Bridget a hateful glare, but holding back from hurling any jibes. Will watched them until they were out of sight then laughed and made a small bow to Bridget.

"Thank you," he said sincerely. "You have taught me another way to fight. Sometimes words make better weapons than fists or swords. Or buckets."

Bridget nodded with a smile. She picked up one of the vessels, hung it on the well hook and began turning the handle to lower it.

"We'd better be quick too," she said. "Cook can be even more frightening than Bragg's master."

Chapter 2: Meetings in the Dark.

They walked together towards the kitchen. Will glanced at Bridget, feeling uneasy that her face still looked hard and cold after their confrontation with Bragg and his lapdogs. She sensed him staring, glanced back and forced a smile.

"You should have left them at the well," Will said. "But I see you're still carrying them." He grinned as he hefted the buckets. "Those three are much heavier then these!"

Bridget made a tutting sound but her smile warmed a little.

"All the Shields are idiots – slow, clumsy giants rattling around in chainmail and tin hats, weighed down by shields as thick as their heads!"

Will chuckled at the venom in her words, but Bridget's mood was softening and then she laughed quietly too.

He said (with a touch of envy he realised), "Shields can take hit after hit and stay on their feet, cutting their way through any enemy. And yes they're slow, but they don't stop. You can't run from them forever."

Bridget shrugged a reply. Will kept staring at her, puzzling over her, amazed again at how compact she was. The top of her head only reached to his nose – and he was considered short compared to most Angalsax boys of his age. She looked harmless, but tonight he had glimpsed something tight-wound inside her; anger, contempt, a swirl of dark emotions. So much energy inside such a little form!

He pressed on with his argument.

"The Shield Wall is part of the best military tactics. You can have all the skirmishers and lobbers you like but it's the Shields that win battles. Their wall stops

patrolling guardsmen. He thought of his errand, of the warband encampment, of one day being a part of it. He found the prospect exciting as reverie crept up on him again…

Will knew that a full warband consisted of about two hundred Shields, sixty lobbers and forty skirmishers: each season the king travelled this way to replace two of the four warbands stationed along the Romani Wall. As usual one warband was drawn from the province's capital and another from the military force of one of Bernicia's inland thegns – men to whom land had been granted by the king. The second warband for this autumn watch were mustered by Thegn Hrodulf and led by his son, Hrothgar. They were not particularly pleased at having to serve at the wall for three months but all warriors in Bernicia had to take their turn…

Will realised he'd been daydreaming again as a figure stepped up beside him with a soft and delicate tread.

"Won't that venison be getting cold?"

The voice, calm and refined, made Will's breath catch such that the platter tilted and the meat began to slide. He caught himself in time, grateful that the near darkness concealed his furious blushes. He bowed, almost spilling the food once again.

"Indeed, yes Princess, I'm sorry, yes, I really must…"

She gave a tinkling laugh at his ramblings; it was a sound that Will loved to hear and could never tire of.

Rowenna, daughter of King Godric, stepped a little closer but kept in the shadow of the longhouse wall. Even so, the pale light of the cloud-hazed moon showed the perfect white teeth of her smile, her golden hair tied up under her flat riding cap and her leather breeches and tunic.

Will realised he was staring. Then concern flashed through him.

"You shouldn't be out here alone, Princess."

She touched his arm and a thrill rippled through him. "But I'm with *you*, Will. And I've told you before you must call me Rowenna – at least when no one else is around. Besides, I can be myself with you and not play at being the stuck up princess."

Will wondered if that was a compliment, or could Rowenna be her ordinary self with him because *he* was so ordinary? He shrugged in reply. Rowenna said, "So what's happened to your face?"

His thoughts flurried. "Oh, just training," Will said lightly, but he knew she could read him well – she must have reckoned what had happened and his heart warmed to her again as she made nothing out of it.

They began to walk together towards the soldiers' encampment, though Will's concern deepened with every step. After a dozen paces he stopped, noting her look of puzzlement.

"Prin – Rowenna. If the soldiers see us together there would be gossip. Or if Osbert…"

His words unravelled like frayed cord. Osbert, Bragg's master, was the king's champion and First Shield of this warband. He was seventeen years older than Rowenna but had made no secret of his affections for her. Will could hardly think of the man without jealousy lancing through him.

"He might come to check whether you are safe."

"You are always looking out for me Will Foundling, and I thank you for it. I understand why you are anxious – but I won't return just yet. I will instead go and see my horse, Wildwind and yourself being my two favourite people."

Will chuckled lightly at that, as Rowenna had intended. She rested her hand on his shoulder briefly, then turned and melted back into the night.

*

It was Guthran who met Will at the edge of the encampment. Will liked him as he was one of the few people who treated him like a human being. Even so, Will's heart beat faster at the thought that he might have seen him with Rowenna, but the man made no mention of it. Instead, clapping Will on the back (so that he nearly dropped the platter), Guthran led him towards the cluster of tents and cookfires where birds, rabbits and other small game hunted that day by the lobbers were sizzling on the spits. The savoury smells made Will's mouth water.

Two men and two women sat around the closest of the fires. Will immediately recognised the older woman – Mildred, the mistress at arms. She looked up and smiled at Will's approach. She, like Guthran, had always been friendly towards him. Also Will admired her because her strength and valour had proved that women could fight equally as well as men, and in Mildred's case even better than most. Her reputation meant that she had been put in charge of training the women and men not deemed tall, strong, skilled or ruthless enough for the shield wall.

Which, for now, included Will.

"Well met Will Foundling," Mildred said in her rich, strong voice. She stood up to take the heavy tray from him. "I hope you

31

haven't been eating this venison on your way over here –"

Her words were cut off as a scream ripped through the night.

Chapter 3: Rescue.

"King's Shields – marching square on me! Skirmishers and lobbers form a perimeter. Hrodulf's warband – half guard for the camp, half follow on!" Cenhelm's voice boomed across the encampment. As the captain of the King's first warband his commands were instantly obeyed. There came the clatter of shields and weaponry being snatched up as the warriors hurried to their positions. Cenhelm, spear and heavy round shield already in hand, strode past Will, leaving Will wondering what he was supposed to do – until the thought flared through his mind that it might have been Rowenna who'd screamed.

Without thinking of his own safety, he took a first frantic step towards the longhouse – until a strong hand grabbed his shoulder and pulled him back.

"Running to hide, nithing? The wall's right here!" Randolph, his face screwed up in disgust, held Will fast. Will cursed his bad luck but could not deny Randolph's accusation with the truth. Admitting that he had been alone outside with Rowenna would throw up all kinds of problems. But then, blessedly, Randolph loosened his grip fractionally, allowing Will to twist free and run headlong towards the longhouse; Randolph's shout of outrage being drowned by the cacophony of noise as Hrodulf's soldiers jumped-to at his stream of orders and began to organise themselves.

Now the air seemed filled with tension, mirroring Will's own taut anxiety. Ahead of him the longhouse door was flung open and the King and his bodyguards or huscarls appeared. As though that were a signal, all of the perimeter fires went out and screeches echoed through the night from every direction, followed by the thud and clatter of arrows and slingshot hitting the longhouse wall and the huscarls' shields as they encircled the King to protect him.

Gods, thought Will, *they'll never get to Rowenna in time even if they know where to look! _And_ assuming they've realised she came outside!*

Panic started to rise in him but with an effort he pushed it aside and drew his own weapon, a seax or shortsword. He was nearing the longhouse now, his meagre plan being to skirt it and then circle the nearby stables in the hope that Rowenna was hiding within. She had a sharp mind and would have reasoned that the brunt of the attackers' arrows would strike at the front of the longhouse first as the soldiers within it emerged.

But the invaders had struck deeper into the settlement than Will had first thought. As he bypassed the longhouse the doors of stable burst open and a man staggered out, an axe driven deep into his chest. It was a

Pict warrior. Another figure appeared a moment later – Osbert, the King's Champion. The Pict half turned as though to defend himself but Osbert was upon him. He kicked the wounded man down on his back and without hesitating plunged a spear straight through his heart. The man shuddered and then, astonishingly, his body crumbled to black ash and spiralled skywards, leaving his clothes, sword and small buckler shield lying in the grass.

Despite his urgency, Will stopped at the sight. He had heard of this transformation before – the Pict gods taking back a dead person's body and soul. But this was the first he had seen of it.

Then Osbert turned to face him, his spear raised.

"No! It's me – Will Foundling!"

He stepped forward as Bragg too came out of the stables followed by Rowenna. The sword she held was dripping with blood. Relief flooded through Will. He held back from running to her but raised a hand as though in greeting.

Then Osbert grabbed the Pict's axe and hurled it at Will.

Will had no time to react. The thought of death touched his mind but then the axe had hurtled past him and thudded into the chest of a second Pict who had been creeping up behind him.

As Will turned to witness again the heavenward swirl of ash his heart sank: another seven enemy warriors, their woad-covered faces a ghastly grey-blue in the moonlight, were charging towards him. Will ignored his first cowardly instinct to run away and his second stupid impulse to stand and fight. Instead he back pedalled towards the stables, diving for the ground only as the attacking Picts hurled their javelins – which swished above Will's body to thud into Osbert and Bragg's heavy shields and the stable walls.

Then the night erupted with battle cries as the Picts broke rank and ran full pelt towards their enemies. One of them slashed his sword at Will as he passed: Will rolled aside then scrambled up. Turning, he saw that Osbert and Bragg had discarded their shields, unusable now with javelins sticking out of them. He and Bragg dispatched the first couple of Picts with hurled spears then drew their swords as the remaining band closed in upon them.

Osbert turned briefly and made to push Rowenna back inside the stable – Will smiled grimly at her gesture of defiance. But then she saw the sense of it and disappeared from view.

Then the close-in, brutal fighting began. The Pict raiders slashed with their swords and jabbed and parried with their small buckler shields. They were screaming and howling constantly, their blood hot with battle fury, careless of their own lives. Osbert and Bragg fought in a more measured way; for them to lose control would bring a rapid death. And it looked for a while as though they could hold back the assault, as the Picts could only come at them two at a time in the doorway. But the sheer frenzy of the attackers and their greater number began to tip the balance. Osbert and Bragg were being forced back into the stable, and once fully inside all five Picts would have space to move and the skirmish would be over. Then the raiders would turn their swords upon Rowenna.

Do something – do something now!

Will's inner voice screamed at him. He ran silently to the rearmost Pict and thrust the seax into the man's broad back. The warrior merely grunted as the nine-inch blade punched in and out of him. He spun around, swinging his sword in a wide arc at head height. Will ducked and slashed the seax across the warrior's thigh. The man staggered to the side, swinging his blade high to cleave Will's skull in two. Will dodged aside as the sword swished past his shoulder and buried itself deep into the earth. Seeing his moment, Will made to strike again as the Pict tried to tug his weapon free – but the man had presence of mind enough to drop to one knee and smashed the metal boss of his buckler into Will's stomach.

Will staggered back and went sprawling to the ground, the wind knocked out of him. He lay stunned as the chaos of battle washed over him like the sea.

"Will – Will watch out!"

Rowenna's voice cut through the yells and death-screams and the unending clash of metal and wood. The Pict, having dragged his sword loose, was advancing again, his grey corpse-like face twisted into a mask of hatred that made him look barely human. Will scrambled to his feet, ignoring the stormtide of pain that swept through his body. He briefly caught sight of Rowenna standing behind Osbert and Bragg, who were still fighting desperately. But exhaustion was showing on their faces. Soon their reactions would slow and they would be hacked down.

He began to scramble to his feet as hope drained out of him to be replaced by bleak despair.

But I won't – I won't give up. I have to try and help Rowenna –

The Pict stopped suddenly and twisted, trying to reach his back. Will saw that Rowenna's seax, skilfully hurled, was lodged between the man's shoulder blades.

Will saw his moment. He rolled forward, steadied himself on one knee and thrust his blade up under the warrior's ribcage.

A wave of heat flowed through the seax and along his arm, then was drawn back to be replaced by numbing cold as the Pict's life energy was sucked out of him. His flesh swiftly blackened and turned to ash that swirled in a vortex skyward as his body and soul returned to their source, his weapons and clothes dropping to the floor.

It was Will's first ever kill. He checked his emotions, but for the present there was only numbness and a small spark of relief that he was still alive. He stooped to retrieve the Pict's sword from among the man's leavings, hefting its weight and struggling with it: although it was well balanced it was too heavy for him to use effectively – he grinned; until he was older and stronger.

A hand clamped his wrist in an iron grip.

"Sword a bit big for you, nithing?" Bragg sneered. He pushed Will's arm away and bent to retrieve Rowenna's seax. Will shook his head but was too tired to argue, soul-sick of confrontation. Instead he looked slowly about himself as the world opened up. Nearby, Osbert was picking among the enemy's leavings for valuables and Rowenna was walking towards him. All of the Picts had gone. Cenhelm's shield wall had formed up in an arc defending the front and side of the longhouse. Thegn Hrodulf's half-shield formation stood fifty feet back, their sword blades and spearpoints glittering in the moonlight. Hrothgar and his captains were just taking their places.

"Skirmishers to the perimeter," Cenhelm shouted, "and get those torches lit. Hrothgar, have your men form up twenty paces back from the trees. Move!"

The men quickly dispersed.

Rowenna came up beside Will, taking back her seax as Bragg held it out to her, hilt foremost.

"Are you all right?" she said softly.

Will bowed his head. "Yes, thank you Princess. I –" The rest of the words caught in his dry throat.

"And thank *you*," she said, and from her belt drew another sword, which she handed to Will. "It is only my practise weapon, but it is well balanced. See how you get on with a shorter blade."

"Rowenna!" Godric's voice boomed across the battlefield. The King, with Will's master Brant Ivenson standing beside him, beckoned his daughter over.

"We'll talk later, Will," she said and with an almost coy smile she left him.

Will's head spun as he realised how close to death he had been in a battle that could only have lasted a few minutes.

Bragg and Osbert were talking quietly close to the stable. Although he might have to suffer the rough edge of Bragg's tongue again, he was determined to be part of the aftermath of the battle; not to be an outsider.

He began to walk over to them when a soldier's voice echoed through the night –

"They've taken the horses. All of them!"

Chapter 4: The Romani Wall.

The two warbands finally marched out of the forest, cresting the ridge to the south of the Romani Wall as the last of the sunlight drained from the sky to the west.

Losing forty horses to the Pict invaders had been serious but not devastating to the King's mission. Angalsax warriors hardly used horses in battle; they were mainly ridden by royals and commanders where the extra height across the field gave an advantage in organising the men. Other than that they were used as pack animals or to pull waggons. In their absence the provisions necessary for the journey from the capital had needed to be distributed among the six hundred soldiers of Godric's entourage; there had been a few quiet grumblings but no open complaints, and little loss of speed.

These thoughts ran through Will's mind as he stood among the quiet crowd. He had read much about the use of cavalry in battle during past times and the devastating effect that mounted warriors had when pitted against foot soldiers. It surprised him that Angalsax commanders had at least not tested the idea by now – but who would listen to the military strategies of an orphan outsider?

Especially now, when rumours had spread that he had run from the shield wall to hide in the dark, only to find himself caught in the midst of the fray. He had told Brant that he'd been heading for the stables, thinking that first scream had come from there (he said nothing about his concerns for Rowenna). Brant had seen no reason to doubt him and Will was grateful for the man's trust and for his company during the journey: he had been about the only one to talk with Will the whole way. Will had also felt uneasy about the reduced range of the scouts as they reconnoitred ahead of the main band. Everyone seemed completely focussed on just reaching the Romani Wall, seemingly not alert enough to the fact that they were moving through dangerous land, clearly proven by the recent Pict attack on the guards.

Will looked along the line hoping to spot Rowenna, but she was not visible in the deepening dark. He hoped that she had at least told the King that he had tried to help. Not that Godric would be much in the mood to listen. He was still furious that such a large Pict raiding party had penetrated so far into Bernicia – a full day's march – without pursuit from the warbands at the Wall. Even more puzzling was the fact that Bernician fighters had not decimated the Pict force before that. The Wall's largest fort, The Anvil, contained ample men to have broken the back of the Pict attack and driven the survivors back into Caledon.

Now the sky had almost emptied of light – just bands of orange and salmon pink away on the left hand horizon and the paltry glow of a first quarter moon high in the south. The darkness was even deeper given that King Godric had ordered all torches to be extinguished before the men moved out of the forest.

Will cast his gaze down into the shadow-filled vale, searching for signs of life. The stillness down there was complete, yet worry moved through him like a cold wind blowing across his heart.

Someone stepped up softly beside him and touched his arm.

"There are no fires," Bridget whispered, her thoughts as uneasy as his.

"No. No torches, nothing. I don't understand it. The Pict raiding party couldn't have been strong enough to overwhelm The Anvil."

"Not on their own," she said nervously, edging a little closer to Will.

He leaned forward to look as far as he could along the Wall, to the west then the east. The silhouette of the great structure reminded him of giant eagle wings brooding over the land. The chronicles said that the Wall had been abandoned two hundred years earlier when its Romani builders had been forced to return to Italia to help shore up their crumbling empire. But it was still as strong as anything the Angalsax could construct now.

A crenulated walkway ran along the top,
which was over three body-heights above
the ground while, directly in front of them,
the Wall ran out southward to form a
rectangular fort.

Will stared hard beyond the fort's
perimeter, scanning for signs of life. A mass
of long, dark barracks and buildings
hunkered around open squares before the
north and south gates. A score or more of

much smaller huts clustered together outside the southern wall. But every window was dark, with not a fire or torch or lamp to be seen. There were supposed to be over two hundred Bernician warriors stationed at the fort alone and the same number of civilians living within and without. Yet now there was no trace of anyone either in the fort or along the battlements, and the thought sprang in Will's mind that death had come there recently and left its mark.

He shuddered, hoping it wouldn't be true.

Chapter 5: What's Out There?

It took less than twenty minutes for the warbands to enter the fort, quickly check the buildings and form up in the Northgate square. Will stood with Brant, who had stationed himself near the royals as usual. Despite the dark mystery and air of tragedy that hung heavily on all present, Will's heart had lifted to catch sight of Rowenna and the secret smile she gave him.

"Since when did Angalsax cower behind locked doors, afraid of the night?" Osbert banged an angry fist against one of the solid wooden outer gates. As the King's Champion he could get away with saying things that ordinary mortals would never dare to. "I say we go out there now and hunt down the savages that did this!"

"No one is afraid," Cenhelm explained, his calm and measured voice in contrast to Osbert's enraged outburst. "Venturing into territory at night that the enemy knows well would make us vulnerable. I think we should secure the fort and wait until morning."

Will nodded approval but said nothing. Earlier he and Brant had quickly checked the fort as the warbands entered and this had given them insight into at least part of what had happened. The nearest watchtower, just three hundred paces along the wall, had obviously been breached. Pict ropes and ladders had been lying on the wall-walk, but there hadn't been many leavings here – clothes and weapons from slain Pict warriors. Brant reckoned the Picts had approached silently, slain the wall guards then launched a full attack against the remaining inhabitants, murdering most of them as they slept. They had only opened the fort gates when there were just a few soldiers to oppose them, but then unaccountably closed them again and pulled up their ladder and ropes.

It looked as though the central square was where the remaining Bernicians had made their last stand. A quick reckoning suggested that almost the entire garrison had been slain, while less than a hundred Pict warriors were killed. Osbert swept his arm across the scene, using this as silent testimony to his point of view.

"We cannot let this go unpunished, Sire. I would like to see swift justice."

Godric sighed heavily. "I agree, though Cenhelm is right and I don't want to risk lives if I can help it. There again, the Picts might be putting distance between us as we stand here undecided, so I suggest a small sortie outside. If we find any Pict living then we will wring from him the truth of what happened here."

"And you will lead the scouting group, I take it?" Osbert locked eyes with the King, but it was he who broke the gaze first. He made a small obedient bow.

Godric said stridently, "Lobbers to the top wall. Huscarls and First Section with me. Cenhelm, have the rest of the Shields ready in the square in case the invaders return." His voice quietened. "Brant, stay close to my daughter. She will no doubt wish to accompany us."

Brant nodded and Will, catching Rowenna's eye again, fell in beside him.

Godric raised his sword high. "Then let's move out!"

*

The wind hit Will as soon as he passed through the gates, blowing in as it did from the north. The column crossed the short bridge across the outer ditch beyond the wall in twos and moved on into the wilds – open grassland dotted with scattered copses whose branches hissed in the gusts, the sound adding to the air of menace that seemed to hang in the night like a fog. Pict tartans and weaponry lay scattered in and around the ditch. Many had died here, but there should surely have been more.

Cenhelm's thirty shield men split into seven groups of four, the outermost two of each group carrying a firebrand. The remaining two Shields stayed close by their Captain. Will kept close to Brant, reassured by the huge man's presence, but as the band explored further he nudged nearer to Rowenna until he could speak quietly to her.

"Princess, this is not the best time, but I did want to thank you for telling the King that I was trying to help, not hide – you know, at the stables."

He was treated to one of Rowenna's disarming and sparkling smiles.

"I spoke the truth. You left the safety of two hundred Shields to find me, armed with nothing but a seax. If others are too stupid to see how brave that was, then they are at fault. But the King believes you and that's what counts. And besides, you fought well –
"

"Even though you had to save *my* life!"

"I've seen how Bragg and others torment you, Will. Estimate yourself more highly," Rowenna said. It sounded like a royal command. "How else will you achieve your ambitions? Besides," she added, as though reading his thoughts, "there are other ways to become a huscarl than by becoming a Shield. I've seen you practising in the woods and I think with more training you would be deadly with a shorter sword and perhaps a small shield, so keep my practise sword. Speed and accuracy are at least as important and necessary as size and strength. How are you finding that shorter blade anyway?"

Will shrugged noncommittally. He appreciated the Princess's faith in him but becoming a Shield had long been his ambition. But for now, he could do nothing, having no money to buy a longer sword. At least because of Rowenna's generosity he had a usable weapon.

Rowenna tapped the two short Romani swords she carried at her hips. "These for instance are superb in tight spaces or –"

"Did you hear that?" Will cut in. "Shouting, like a child's voice."

Others had heard it too, so that very quickly warriors moved up to form a protective circle around Rowenna, the King and those nearest to them.

Then everyone fell silent, their eyes straining into the dark, weapons readied in case of attack.

The voice came again and closer now.

"Wait – Angalsax. Friends here. Help us!"

"Stay alert," Godric said. "This could be a trick."

Will used a trick of his own; shutting his left eye and, making a tunnel of his curled fingers, looked through it with the right, thus instantly improving his night vision.

"I see them," Will said as he peered between the Shields' shoulders. "A boy and a smaller girl, running together. They're holding hands."

"Signs of anyone else?" said Brant. "I see the children myself now…"

"No one else I think."

Brant broke rank and stepped towards
the running figures. The girl stopped dead at
the sight of this towering Scandian standing

before her with his massive axe blade raised and glinting in the torchlight. She tugged the boy to a halt.

"Step closer so I can see you better." Brant said. They obeyed, and now others could see that these strangers were just what they appeared to be, two filthy frightened children, both with pale skin and red hair typical of the Picts. The boy, who was perhaps ten years old, jabbed frantically back the way they had come and jabbered something in Pictish, then more haltingly in Angalsax – "They here. They here! Get behind the walls."

"What's coming?" Godric said.

Brant stepped beyond the forward line and shouted back, "He's right. I see something. It's coming fast."

"What's out there?" Godric demanded to know.

The child, shivering with terror, opened his mouth to speak.

Chapter 6: A Fury of Teeth and Claws.

"Wolves!" yelled Brant. "Forty paces away and coming fast. Thunor's Hammer they're the size of ponies. And by the gods they're all around us! Make fire – light more torches now!" The torchbearers quickly obeyed, pulling unlit firebrands from their belts and touching them into flame.

The little Pict girl let out a trembling scream. Rowenna said, "Father let them come behind the Shields." And, seeing Godric's hesitation she added, "They might have valuable knowledge about what's going on here."

Reluctantly the King nodded and the two nearest Shields made way for the children to pass.

A moment later something huge streaked out from behind a clump of gorse, a fury of dagger sharp teeth and claws and bristling black fur. The creature let out a guttural roar and smashed into the Shield Wall. Men staggered back under the force of it, barging into Will and Rowenna. Will drew his seax blade, smiling with grim irony at the conversation he had just had with the Princess.

The men that had been struck locked their shields together again and braced themselves.

"Wolves are not stupid," Will said. "They know better than to attack armed warriors –"

The Pict boy tugged at his sleeve. "Not wolves. Vargs. They vargs."

Will and Rowenna exchanged glances. Vargs were things of myth and legend; they didn't really exist. *Except*, thought Will, *they obviously do!*

The creatures were circling the shield wall looking for any chink or weakness. Seeing none, they attacked anyway, hurling their weight against the tops of men's shields, dragging them down to reach the warriors behind. Terrified screams added to the cacophony of growling and roars as men began to die swiftly but horribly. One of the vargs swept a second-row soldier aside with a swipe of its huge paw, leaving Will, Rowenna and the children exposed.

Instinct rather than tactics dictated what happened next –

As the animal lunged at Will, its jaws wet with saliva and spattered blood, he snatched up a torch and thrust it into the creature's face. The Pict boy drove his seax into the varg's paw as Rowenna, sidestepping Will, plunged her twin Romani blades into the creature's chest. The varg stiffened and the red rage drained from its eyes. As it collapsed two Shields pushed it away, a dead weight.

Gods, we can't hold out for much longer!

Nearby, Osbert was fighting desperately at the King's side. They stood with the second row Shields now, stabbing and hacking at any vargs that broke through the ranks of the foremost warriors. It was effective positioning, but even so vargs were getting past forcing Will, Rowenna and the children to fight for their lives.

Will grabbed another firebrand and held it high to give the Shields nearby more light.

Small fragments of burning rag dropped onto his bare arms as rock-hard, sweating backs buffeted against him. He stumbled and slipped over blood, mud and the trampled leavings of dead Angalsax as he tried desperately to see between the jostling, tightly packed warriors.

Then a howl, shrill and haunting, sliced through the din of the battle.

"They call for more," the Pict boy yelled. "More vargs come!"

"Hold the wall!" Godric shouted. "Left wheel then stay together as we make for the fort. Now!"

The men moved flawlessly to obey, trained as they were in every conceivable battle manoeuvre. They positioned themselves in line such that Godric and Osbert, Will, Rowenna and the children were facing the fort, then set up a controlled, steady march towards the refuge. Will passed a second torch to the boy then stooped to grab a fallen spear, which gave him a little more confidence than his seax.

And now he could hear shouts of encouragement from the fort battlements as Cenhelm's warriors poured out through the gates and over the bridge, forming up to make a corridor like a mother's arms outstretched. Will reckoned that with these extra men they would all have a fighting chance, except that they were still two hundred paces away.

Suddenly three vargs leapt at the Shield Wall together. They sprang high, bringing down two men. Godric was flung to the ground, dragging at the Shield next to him so that the man staggered off balance. A varg was upon him instantly, its jaws closing on his throat, bringing swift and bloody death. His body burst into a cloud of black specks that spiralled upwards. Other warriors stabbed and hacked at the creature until it lay still.

Now there was a gap in the line. Will sprang forward without thinking, snatching up a shield and holding that and his spear as he had seen the Shields do.

The formation had come to a halt. Men helped Godric up and now he called loudly, "Close shields!"

Woden's blood, I'm in the front line!

The thought rang through Will's mind as the soldiers slammed together again almost crushing him.

Two vargs hurtled in from the side, one of them leaping straight at Will. He thrust with his spear but the creature was fast and he stabbed empty air. The animal crashed into him, knocking him down; it felt like a wall had collapsed onto his body. Then once again a monstrous animal face was close to his, its roars deafening, its jaws gaping wide. The stink of its breath was sickening.

Nearby soldiers hacked and stabbed at the thing. The varg looked up and rather than try to fight back, made to leap away from the danger – straight at Rowenna, Will realised.

As the creature's weight came off him, Will grabbed at a rear leg. Then he screamed. It felt like his arm was being torn from its socket. Pain raged through his body but he held on with every grain of determination he possessed. It was enough. The varg gave up its lunge for the Princess and instead twisted round to turn its fury on Will, trying to savage his arm. Warriors quickly dispatched it.

"Stay out of the lines," one of the men snapped at him.

The formation was shifting now, on the move again. Will started to scramble painfully up, when two arms slipped under his shoulders and hauled him to his feet.

"Walk, Will." Rowenna's voice rose high and clear above the noise of battle. "Just walk. Walk with me."

He was only too glad to do so. His heart was still hammering with the danger he'd faced and the death that had come so close to him this night. And he felt exhausted, battle-weary, as pain lanced and throbbed through his flesh.

The strange, ululating howl that they had all heard before came again, to be answered a moment later more distantly by another.

"We must run!" The Pict boy's voice called out from somewhere to Will's left. "Now the big pack come!"

Will turned to look back and saw at least fifty of the creatures pour out from between the trees and come bounding towards the formation. But the Shields that remained were the best of Godric's warband, including the fact that faced with these odds they were not dismayed, but roared back at the charging beasts, finding extra courage from somewhere to redouble their efforts at the vargs' renewed attack.

Will caught sight of Osbert fighting savagely at the King's side. It was an inspiring sight. Now the Shields were working as one unit, cutting the vargs down. As Godric slew another of the animals, he gave the command for the formation to move more quickly. The vargs came on again, trying to harry the front line. But now the scene was brighter with the torchlight from the battlements, and the yells from Cenhelm's men were nearer but almost drowned out by the clash of their swords on their shields.

Then, as though sensing that the balance had tipped, the remaining vargs suddenly broke off, turned tail and bounded back towards the forest, some of them tumbling dead or wounded to the ground as archers firing from the battlements found their mark.

Godric, his face weary but triumphant, led his men along the corridor of steel and safely through into the fort. When the last Shield was in, Brant and the other huscarls slammed the great doors shut. The cheering died away and stunned silence filled the courtyard.

Chapter 7: In the Feast Hall.

The discussion in the feast hall had turned into heated bickering as the situation across the kingdom was assessed. Many soldiers whose nerves were still ragged in the aftermath of the varg attack had drunk far too much ale. Their tempers were high and loudly voiced opinions had taken the place of reasoned argument. Aside from that, Godric had decided to send Rowenna with a small band of companions for protection back to Yeavering. They would walk along the Romani Wall to the River Fort and then sail downstream to the capital. With hostile Pictish forces only a day's march south of the fort, the day-and-a-half boat journey meant that the Princess would arrive in time to deliver a warning of the imminent attack. Godric and his warbands would follow on by foot, hopefully completing the six-day march in time to engage with the Picts before they struck. Those were the bones of the plan.

Information about what the enemy tribes were up to had come from the Pict boy Donal, son of the head of his clan. In his halting Angalsax (occasionally lapsing into Pictish, which some of the assembly understood and translated) he explained that all of the Pictish tribes except his own had stormed The Anvil and then moved on south. He also revealed that the vargs were creations of the druids – loregivers and spellweavers; wolves transformed by dark blood-magic that allowed the druids to control them. One or two druids must have died during the battle and with their spellwork unwoven the vargs under their thrall would be free to run wild.

"But why are your people uniting against us?" Alphage, Wyatt's master, wanted to know.

"The druids push other tribes to war. With lands torn by conflict, druids can more easily wield their power. They are sly. They spread their evil secretly. But my father said no and so the other clans attack us. Many died so that I and my sister Effie could escape. We –"

Osbert's growl of outrage cut him short.

"Don't play us for fools, boy. All of your people are the same – savages! For all we know you were sent to spy on us."

"Spy for whom?" Godric said reasonably. "The Picts are on their way to Yeavering. That's a crisis – and you want to kill children?"

"*He* says they move south." Osbert jabbed an accusing finger at Donal but at the King's warning scowl he let the matter drop.

"I know this lad," the King said, "from meetings with his father, the Selgovae clan are – were – decent enough. They traded with us fairly for ten years and kept peace all that time. I intend to let him accompany Rowenna so that he can tell our people at Yeavering everything he knows about the invasion –"

Godric's announcement sparked another round of rowdy disagreement.

"Enough!" the King roared, banging is fist on the long wooden table. The men quietened sullenly. "My mind is set on that. It only remains now for me to decide who will accompany Donal, Effie and my daughter."

*

A few moments later the kitchen doors flew open and the apprentices on serving duty, which included Will tonight, stepped into the feast-hall carrying fresh flagons of ale, roasted meats and salted tubers on large platters. The mood in the room lifted immediately.

"Will Foundling," boomed a voice as Will appeared. "The Princess tells me that you deserve a drop of that ale yourself."

Will turned and his mouth dropped open to realise that it was the King himself who had spoken. He bowed as low as he could given the burden of the ale jugs he carried. Those sitting close to Godric, all Shields, muttered their disapproval. Will's thoughts whirled confusedly. He had no idea what to do. Only royals and elites sat at the high

table. He wouldn't dare to sit among them –
but would it be appropriate for him to
interrupt his serving to take a place
elsewhere in the hall to drink?

After a few moments' hesitation he
bowed again and hurried up on to the dais
where the King's table stood. When he
poured more ale for the King, perhaps
Godric would advise him further on the
etiquette of the matter. But as he approached
his foot caught on something and he had to
slam one of the jugs down on the table to
prevent himself from falling.

Laughter erupted from nearby tables; the
hard men of the Shield Wall liked nothing
better than to see an outsider-apprentice fail.
Will took a calming breath and straightened,
trying not to look at Rowenna.

"Watch where you put your clumsy feet, urchin," said a sneering voice. "Look, you've slopped beer on the table here."

It was Wyatt, an acolyte of Woden and someone who had despised Will from the start. Will saw him slowly withdraw his foot back beneath the table. Wyatt grinned maliciously.

Will kept his temper with an effort. Putting the jugs down gently he pulled a cloth from his belt and dabbed at the spilled beer.

"Quickly," Wyatt snapped, "else it'll spill on my holy robes !"

Will gave a small deferential bow. Wyatt was a powerful man who would likely become High Cleric one day. It would be very unwise to provoke him.

As Will continued mopping the spillage, more laughter burst from the crowd. At the far end of the table Puck, the King's jester, was in the process of miming Will's unfortunate stumble. His long willowy body flipped into a roll, bringing him close to Will as he stood.

"Your cloth is sodden, young Foundling. Here take mine." Another cloth appeared in Puck's hand as though by magic. Despite the situation, Will had to smile as the jester's sleight-of-hand drew gasps from those nearby. While Puck was commonly called the Fool, Will knew him to be highly intelligent and clever. His little theatrical show had shifted the mood of the assembly: the men were chuckling now as they discussed how Puck could have performed his trick.

Puck bowed to the crowd and the men banged their ale jugs on the tables to show their appreciation of the entertainment. And under cover of all this, Will pretended to trip again, thrusting his ale jugs at Wyatt but stopping before any liquid could slosh out. He had caught some of Puck's mischievousness but knew too that Wyatt wouldn't want to cause a scene now that the men's mood had been lifted.

Puck had seen what had happened. He took one of the jugs from Will and led him by the hand towards the King. "Be careful youngling. One day Wyatt will take his revenge if you go too far."

"Not like you to trip over your own feet," Godric said as Will came up to him.

No. They were Wyatt's cursed feet!

"It's been a long day, Sire," Will said. He bowed and began filling the King's ale jug.

Godric nodded. "Aye. And anyone can trip and fall. It's how you get up that counts. And who helps you, or not." He raised a quizzical eyebrow. "Despite the gossip, I hear from Brant that you did well today. And my daughter tells me you fought off a varg with fire as it attacked the two of you."

"Yes Sire, but it was R – it was the Princess's blades that finished off the beast."

Close by, Osbert gave a derisive laugh, spraying fragments of food as he did so. "I wonder if you could have slain the creature anyway, with your torches and lady-sword!"

"I did what I could with what was available." Will kept a respectful tone to his words. "And, sir, I strive to better myself every day, to serve King Godric and the Princess as best I can. I hope to earn a place in the Shield Wall one day…"

Will's jaws snapped shut. His last words might have been designed to give Osbert yet another opportunity to mock him. But before he could, Will turned back to the King and finished filling his jug. As he did so he caught sight of Bridget stepping up on to the dais with platters piled with more food. And he saw Wyatt's foot slide out from under the table again.

"Bridget – watch out –"

But the warning wasn't needed. Bridget stopped dead, one foot lifted and in the perfect position to stamp down on Wyatt's toes and break them. She looked challengingly at the man for a moment, then smiled sweetly, hopped over his outthrust foot and placed the food platters before the King, bowing nervously. As she stepped away she bumped into Will. He steadied her gently.

"My hero," she whispered with the flicker of a smile. Then, more loudly, "Cook wants you to bring out more ale."

"And be quick about it!"

Will sighed. Osbert always needed to have the last word.

"But before you do," Godric said, pushing his goblet towards Will. "Take your drink lad. You did your best to protect Rowenna, putting yourself in danger twice in two days. You've earned it."

Will sipped the dark, thick liquid, not particularly liking the flavour. But to be invited to sup from the King's own mug was an honour indeed.

"Thank you Sire," he said. "This is a great reward for just doing my duty."

The King's lips curved into an almost sympathetic smile.

"You might not thank me for my second 'reward' to you…"

Chapter 8: Along the Wall.

Will's head was still reeling from the King's command – to send him as one of Rowenna's protectors on her journey to the capital. Godric's decision had sent ripples of dissent through the feast hall, though no one had dared to speak out openly, not even the elites at the high table. And not even Wyatt, who despised Will perhaps more than anyone else.

He had quickly packed a bag (Puck advised him to take only what he could run with) and joined the group on the battlements. As soon as the scouts returned and reported the way was clear, they set out for River Fort.

As they walked, Will reflected on his mixed and complex emotions. He was honoured and delighted to be chosen by the King (and to be so close to Rowenna!), but here he was now out in the freezing cold, having left the safety of The Anvil, travelling with a company of warriors who doubted his value among them. And he was sure that vargs still roamed the land, whether under druid control or not. *And* the Picts might have anticipated a Bernician mission by river to warn the people of Yeavering, leaving scouts of their own scattered along the banks.

Will sighed, drew his cloak more tightly about himself and put his head down into the brunt wind.

At the time of their departure, another party had set off westward along the wall to the section guarded by Reghed, a neighbouring Celtic kingdom a day's hard march away. The men had been carrying torches and remained in plain sight as a diversionary tactic if any Picts or druids were watching the wall. Will's group had needed to move in darkness, crouching low to keep their heads below the battlements. Striding along bent double had soon caused Will's back to scream with pain, but after a few hissed warnings from Iver, one of

Osbert's lobbers, for him to keep up, Will had resigned himself to the discomfort and danger and kept close behind Donal and Effie, whom he had been tasked with guarding. Aside from himself, Rowenna, the Pict children and Iver, the party included Puck and thirteen other men, all hand picked for their stamina and fighting prowess.

After the group had been crouch-jogging for an hour, the signal came back that it was safe to stand. Will straightened up gratefully, his backbone crackling. A languorous warmth spread through his muscles as normal blood flow returned. He tried to catch sight of Rowenna, but her golden hair was covered by a dark shawl. He easily spotted Brant however, whose instructions had been to keep no more than a pace away from the Princess the whole time.

The warrior's huge frame and the silhouette of his great double-headed axe were reassuring. Will found himself smiling at that, and at his mental picture of Rowenna –

Well, if I can't see her in the flesh...

Now the men were bunching up so that their number could not be so easily calculated by any enemy that spotted them. And they set up the pace for the rest of their journey to River Fort, a striding jog that left Will breathless early on, though he found it was manageable once he'd got his second wind.

Every few minutes he glanced out over the land, ghostly pale in the moonlight. At first he had been trying to spot any movement, but Pict or druid or any vargs they controlled would be sure to keep to the shadows. Nor was there any sign of unleashed vargs – not that the thought made Will feel any safer. Anything but. There had not been a full Pict invasion for almost fifty years. Most of the thegns from the south and west of the kingdom had long believed that the threat was over, and that maintaining a heavily armed border wall was a waste of resources. Well, they had been proved decisively wrong in one sense: four entire warbands spread over Bernicia's forty-mile section of wall hadn't managed to stop the Picts at all. Will wondered if any Angalsax had survived, reflecting that a border force of even double the strength would have been hard put to repel the Pict attack.

When the moon was much lower in the sky the party stopped, huddling in the shelter of a watchtower out of the wind. Waterskins were unhitched from belts and the travellers quenched their thirsts. Some of the men chewed on strips of dried salted meat.

Now as Will craned forward in hope, he caught sight of Rowenna. She had pushed back her hood to drink and converse with Brant and the other men. She was smiling and laughing with them and Will thought (yet again!) that she was the most beautiful girl he had ever seen. Then she happened to glance his way and her smile broadened. She mouthed 'Are you all right?' and Will nodded eagerly.

"Your head'll fall off boy!"

The coarse voice at his ear made him jump. The comment had come from Alston, the second of the two lobbers – the other being Iver – who had been running rearguard behind him.

"Just stretching." Will stood and kept his tone amicable, ignoring Alston's sneer and Iver's oafish grin. He kept the spear he was holding tilted downwards so that Alston would not think he wanted to fight.

"I'm sure." Alston jabbed him in the chest. "You're getting' way above your station, nithing, if you fancy yourself as the Princess's little protector like your master. Besides that you're a weakling, she should have her own kind watchin' over her."

"We're all here to see her safely back to Yeavering." Will kept his voice steady, wanting to show that they had their mission in common. The two lobbers had now been joined by two more, Wilfred and Wilfor, dangerous men all of them; deadly with any missile and battle-hardened against Picts and Scandian sea-raiders.

Suddenly Iver thrust out his hand and took Will's arm in an iron grip.

"Steady on there lad. You looked as though you were losing your balance."

"And we don't want that, do we?" Alston took a pace closer and grabbed Will's other arm. "Wouldn't do for you to slip and fall off this ol' wall."

"But accidents do happen," said Wilfor, his voice thin and reedy. He glanced at the twelve-yard drop on the Caledon side. "As they will for your little savage friends. They don't belong up here either."

Will snatched a breath to cry for help but the lobbers had him, shoving him over the edge before he could make a sound.

Chapter 9: Fall from Grace.

Will dropped his spear as he toppled backwards and instinctively grabbed at whatever was in reach, which was the haft of one of Alston's throwing axes. He hauled himself upright but then Wilfred pushed him back again as Alston peeled his fingers off the axe. Desperately Will fought against them as his feet scrabbled on the damp stone, one foot slipping over the edge and into empty air. With a huge effort he swung it back and tried to hook his leg around Alston's ankle, but Iver kicked it free.

Suddenly a shadow dropped out of the night and landed lithely beside him. The figure gripped Alston's hand, effortlessly twisted it free and swung him round so that now *he* teetered on the edge of the wall.

Warm gratitude flooded through Will as he recognised Puck. The jester had jumped from the tower top a body length above them. Whether he had sensed trouble or had simply been on watch Will didn't know. Not that it mattered – two against four were much better odds.

"Shall we dance?" Puck smiled at Alston and the others, but the smile was steely and challenging. Will wondered again at the depths of the man: scratch the fool and underneath you found strength, intelligence and a blessed sense of justice. He broke free of Alston's grip as Puck carried out some strange but clever manoeuvre that flipped Alston around and sent him tumbling into Iver, sending both men crashing to the ground. Then Puck stood with legs apart and well balanced should any of the lobbers come at him.

"Very impressive," he said to Alston. "An acrobat as well as a thuggish bully. Are there no end to your talents?"

Just then Osbert burst out through the tower door.

"What by the gods is all the noise out here?" he demanded to know, staring disdainfully at the lobbers scrambling back to their feet. Puck made a grovelling bow: Will smiled inwardly at the man's show of sarcasm.

"Just having a dance to keep the muscles supple, master." Puck's face broke into a huge grin. "So that we might keep up with you in the running."

Osbert glared at all of them, his expression hardening as he looked at Alston.

"You're meant to lead these idiots," he snarled. "And you should know well by now that even low-life lobbers are not meant to mix with outsiders!"

"Yes sir. It won't happen again." The hatred-filled glance he gave Will suggested it would.

"Useless hurlers," Osbert sneered. "At least the skirmishers have done their job – the fort is clear." He grabbed the twins and pushed them into the tower. "Now get back in line. We're moving again."

Osbert stormed back into the tower.

With a surprisingly strong grip, Puck guided Will through the tower and out of the door on the far side. Will muttered his thanks to the jester for his help as he tried to ignore the muffled curses from the men behind him.

*

Will thought that the pre-dawn sky was very beautiful, as clear as glass and filled with early light. He looked back along the wall that they had travelled; it stretched away sharply uphill into a dawn groundmist that was slowly rising with the temperature. Will was glad they were not going in *that* direction.

The company had made good progress and were now resting again at another of the towers. Will had noted that Puck was keeping a fatherly eye on him, and he was grateful for that. But Alston and the others had not troubled him further. Having glimpsed the jester's steel beneath the sheath of his tomfoolery, they would think twice before stirring up any more trouble.

Suddenly Wilfor's voice cut through the men's murmured conversations and the stillness of the morning. He gestured from his vantage point atop the tower.

"A runner. A runner from the west!" His brother joined him and they quickly nocked arrows to their bows.

Brant appeared at the door. He made as though to keep Rowenna inside and behind him, but she gently put his arm aside and moved past him. Her armoured guards stayed close.

"All lobbers to the roof," she commanded. "One of you check the other directions. This could be a diversion."

Wilfred disappeared from view. Wilfor braced himself by placing one foot on the crenelated wall. Moments later Alston and Iver joined him, bows at the ready.

Now Will could see the figure about a hundred paces away moving quickly along the wall, though its gait was unsteady on the dew-damp stone. He glanced up to see the three lobbers take aim, drawing their bowstrings back to their ears.

"But what if it's a messenger, a friend..." Will muttered this half to himself as Osbert barged roughly past him, followed by Bragg who stood by his master. They raised their shields, locked them and levelled their spears over the top.

"Lobbers ready," Osbert growled.

"Aye, First," came Alston's reply.

Brant edged in front of Will, glancing at him briefly. "Spear!" he snapped.

Will raised his spear ready although he couldn't imagine how one small runner could fight its way past Osbert and Bragg.

"On my word," Osbert's clear commanding voice rang out.

One _small_ runner...

The figure looked up.

"Wait!" Will yelled. "I know who it is!"

Chapter 10: Close Every Door To Me.

The sun rose directly ahead of them, turning the mist into a thick shining veil.

"It's not burning off," Will gasped as he ran close behind Bridget. "The moisture in the air is making it thicker. I can't see a thing."

"As long as you can see the edge," she called back to him, chuckling. He grinned at her show of humour despite her exhaustion. She had run from The Anvil to catch up with Rowenna's party bringing a warning that not all of the Picts had travelled south. At least a hundred of them and many druid-controlled vargs had remained and, learning of the Princess's mission to the capital, had set out to stop it. Battle-seasoned runner that she was, Bridget's energy was almost gone and Will now feared for her safety if she should fall behind the others.

A disembodied howl rose through the glowing white wall around them and was answered by three more.

"They're getting too damned close," Alston said, running ten paces behind

Bridget and Will. He let out a string of curses –

If he fought as well as he swore we'd get through this!

But Will didn't bother to reply: words wasted precious air.

"Go faster you lazy scum or I'll hurl you both off the wall!"

Alston had come up close behind them, sorely tempting Will to jab backwards with his spear. But the lobber was right, they needed to move as fast as they possibly could. Will picked up his pace, his leg muscles feeling as though they were on fire. Groaning, Bridget followed suit.

They had been running for an hour since Bridget joined them, and now Will had fallen behind. But by his reckoning the next tower should be coming up soon, bringing them all brief sanctuary and the chance to rest. Then to Will's great relief Bridget's voice rang out ahead of him and moments later the square bulk of the tower loomed through the mist. She barged the door aside without slowing and, as Will entered, slumped against the far wall dragging for breath. Will joined her. Alston and the other three lobbers staggered in behind him. Iver slammed the door shut and rammed its iron bolt into place.

Will went over and helped the lobbers drag a heavy table across and up-end it against the door as an extra precaution.

Will slouched back across the room and eased himself down again beside Bridget. She smiled at him wearily and his heart gladdened that he was with her again. Despite the way they sometimes irritated one another, Will had always felt close to Bridget. He patted her arm and her smile broadened as though similar thoughts were in her mind. As one of Tolan's top battle-runners she had been sent with two skirmishers to warn Rowenna and her party of the Picts' stratagem – over a hundred of them had overrun The Anvil and a large number now were in pursuit both along and beside the wall. As she told Will now, it had only been because the skirmishers had stayed behind to buy her time that she managed to reach him.

"There's no way they could have survived," she said quietly with a catch in her voice, causing Will's thoughts to deepen –

So did the Pict gods prevent the Angalsax gods from saving those men? Why do the gods let all of this death and violence happen anyway? What's the damned point of them!

He said nothing of this but simply let Bridget work through her moment of sadness.

Shortly afterwards the lobbers struggled wearily to their feet and Iver indicated that it was time to move on. By common agreement and heeding Osbert's advice they and Will had decided to let the main party run on while they secured each tower they came to. The vargs, faster and with more stamina than humans, would need to wait until the Picts caught up and smashed through each tower's doors. Will felt dismayed at this but comforted himself with the thought that Rowenna and her men would be at least two towers ahead of them by now.

They set off once more. Glancing over the Pictish side of the wall, Will saw vargs keeping pace with them. The Picts would not be very far behind.

"At least they can't get up here," he gasped. "And the next tower isn't too far away." But Will knew as well as Bridget that this was cold comfort. Even as they'd hurried away from the last tower they'd heard the howl of the vargs at the eastern door, and then the thunderous crash and battering as the Pict warriors smashed at the oak with their axes and battle-hammers.

The minutes dragged by in an agony of straining limbs and scalding lungs. Will had fallen back to match Bridget's slower pace, but Iver was having even more difficulty keeping up and this caused Will's worry to deepen – doubly so as the other three lobbers, running ahead and mere grey shadows in the mist, would reach the tower first. Will wouldn't put it past them to lock the door against him and Bridget and Iver if the enemy gained ground.

He found himself trapped in the dilemma. He had been counting paces since the last tower and thought that now they were just a couple of hundred from the next. He dearly wanted to help Bridget but his dark thoughts about Alston and the others clawed at his mind. So, raising a placating hand to her, Will increased his speed until he was running just a couple of paces behind the lobbers –

And instantly regretted it as they all heard the howl of vargs behind them on the wall. The Picts had smashed through the tower doors already!

But now the bulky silhouette of the next tower appeared ghost-like through the mist.

Alston put on an extra burst of speed and rammed open the door. Wilfor and Wilfred hurtled in after him and then, to Will's horror, began to close it after them. Yet there was only fear on his face and not the malicious grin that Will might have expected.

Will raced on then threw himself at the door, barging it open against Alston's weight.

"You'll get us all killed!" the lobber yelled, but Will ignored that, using all his strength to keep the door ajar until Bridget and then a staggering Iver stumbled past him and were safe. Will stood aside. Alston crashed the door closed and shot the bolt.

"Gods save us," he gasped and Will smiled grimly at his earlier thoughts.

Maybe the gods are having their revenge because I criticised them!

Something huge and heavy slammed into the oak, followed by the sounds of the stout panels being clawed. Seconds later came the thud and booming of the Picts' weapons.

"We can't rest here," Alston said urgently. He swept his gaze over Iver and then at the twins. "Get up on the roof Iver – you two help him if he hasn't the strength."

The man's eyes filled with terror.

"You'll never make it to the next fort. You've no strength left," Alston said reasonably. "You have a better chance up there than trying to run. Close and bolt the trapdoor. You can shoot down at them. Maybe they'll give up on you to keep coming after us. It's an order."

Iver nodded dumbly and moved towards the tower steps.

Will shot a glance at Bridget.

"Can you manage another run? Or…" He found he could not speak the alternative.

With a splintering crackle one of the door's oak planks split apart. A Pict axe-head worried at it, opening the gap. More chunks flew free. But then there came a human cry as Iver scored his first hit.

"Let's go," Alston said. They closed the second door and ran.

The only thought sustaining Will now as he slogged behind Bridget was that the next fort was the last one. From there they could take to the river. The prospect of possible escape cheered him momentarily, his mood sinking again as they all heard Iver's agonised scream behind them. The man's life had bought them a few precious minutes.

Seemingly a lifetime later the River Fort came into view. Will knew that Rowenna and her party would most likely have boats waiting, together with the manpower to fight off the enemy. He was about to make the point to Bridget when a slingshot struck his back. Will let out an agonised yell. Simultaneously, stone fragments flew up beside him while crossbow bolts clattered nearby.

"Come on – come on!" Will shouted through the pain, as much to stir himself as the others.

But now the door was just a blessed ten paces ahead and with a last giant effort Will reached it, scrabbled for the latch and pushed.

The door didn't move.

Chapter 11: New Legs.

"No!" Will screamed his horror and outrage but realised he was panicking. He put his weight against it more calmly and the door gave a little, then flew open with a screech. Strong arms grabbed him, spun him through and then hauled Bridget in as she staggered the final few paces. The door was pushed closed and bolted.

"Idiots!" called Alston from the open trapdoor above. "You could have let the beasts –"

The leading varg crashed against the oak and Will had to admit that Alston had a point. He glanced round to see who had helped him, managing an exhausted smile as Puck jumped in mock terror at the varg's arrival.

"Step back from it all," the jester said. His tone was kindly. "And Bridget too. Join us when you're rested. We have to hold this tower for a while."

"Where's everyone else? Is Rowenna –"

"They're down in the repair yards on the other side of the bridge, looking for a vessel that's serviceable. If there aren't any we'll all have to swim to Yeavering." Puck noted Will's brief startlement and grinned. "Keep a lookout. When they're ready the Princess will send someone to signal. Then we can leave."

He nodded towards a small, shuttered window opposite, then snatched a long stave from the shadows by the door and leaped lightly up the steps leading to the tower top. Will heard an inhuman shriek beyond the door and Wilfor's shocked but triumphant cry from above –

"Got it! But the brute nearly reached me."

Will moved stiffly to the window. Bridget joined him but slumped down to sit.

138

She drew her knees up and wrapped her arms about them, letting her head sag.

"I didn't know Puck could use a weapon," Will said.

"There's plenty you don't know about him. But know this – don't assume he's your friend just because he hasn't killed you yet. That man's thoughts run deeper than the river."

"But he's just saved our lives – mine for a second time."

Bridget shrugged, glancing up at Will. "I wonder why, given he's barely acknowledged your existence at court these past couple of years."

"Maybe because we're all here together fighting for our lives –"

Alston's voice roared from the tower top as the cacophony of varg snarls and raking at wood died away. "Filthy curs, they're running!"

"Only until the Picts arrive to break down the door for them. Then they'll risk our arrows and slingshot again." Will pointed to the big table in the middle of the room. "Come on, give me a hand with this."

Bridget stood stiffly and with a groan and together they laboriously managed to drag the table across the room and upend it against the eastern door. Then Will returned to the window opposite and gazed out. At last the sun was burning off the worst of the mist and from his vantage point he could see the wall spanning the swiftly flowing river. It was at least two hundred yards across, its swirling waters the colour of hammered lead. But there was no sign of Rowenna or the others, nor indeed of any boats. The moorings were empty.

Without warning a thunderous clattering filled the room as a hail of flung stones struck the far door.

"The Pict lobbers are here," Bridget said needlessly. They both knew that now it was just a matter of time before the enemy gained access. In his mind's eye Will saw the stormtide of vargs and behind them the demon-faced Pict warriors charging towards him and Bridget. And then death would be swift but agonising.

Bridget hurried across and peered through the shuttered window beside the door. She said nothing but Will saw her shoulders slump as she read defeat at the sheer number of the enemy.

"They're charging again," yelled a voice from the tower top. Will recognised it as Gwen's – *So not just lobbers up there. Rowenna really does want this tower guarding.* Knowing she was there reassured him a little, for Gwen was a superb scout and truly gifted in close-quarter combat.

The sonorous notes of blaring war trumpets filled the air, a signal to rally the Picts and strengthen their hearts. Even before the sound fell away, Puck yanked open the trapdoor and hurriedly beckoned Will and Bridget to join him.

"This will be their most concerted attack," the jester said. "Let our bowmen and lobbers do their work. Keep watch on the trapdoor and look out for slingstones and crossbow bolts."

They both nodded. But even as they reached the trap door they heard the splintering scream of oak planks torn asunder and the mighty crash of the table they'd shifted toppling over.

Moments later there came a series of bangs from beneath the trapdoor and although it held the hinges screeched upwards half a finger length out of the stone. Will's instinct was to jump on it to see if his weight would push the hinge bolts back down – but Bridget read his intention and pulled him away.

"Don't be stupid. You could get a sword blade through your foot!"

He was about to argue that this was no time to play safe, but now Bridget was looking past him, her eyes wide with horror. Will spun round and mirrored her expression.

Incredibly, impossibly, what looked like a bloated black hand with too many fingers was creeping over the wall between two merlons on the northern, river, side.

How had the thing climbed up the sheer wall? And what was it anyway?

Will's imagination struggled to picture the creature to which the hand belonged – but then it emerged fully and the reality was worse than any vision he could have woven.

A spider, bigger than anything Will had ever seen, remained for a moment on the wall, its mandibles and forelimbs questing as it sensed its prey, then it dropped to the floor with a heavy plop and came scuttling towards them.

Will let out a groan of disgust. The thing was fast and looked deadly. Its eight skeletal legs held its bulbous body a foot off the floor. Will drew his sword as the spider leapt but had no time to strike.

Instinctively he turned away and felt the creature's wiry hairs brush across his face. It hit the floor beyond him with a soft thud. And then Will did strike, plunging his sword blade into the mass of the thing. Black ichor squirted and the legs thrashed frantically. But most horribly it let out a keening cry that died away a moment before all movement stopped.

The others on the tower top had been preoccupied with the Pict and varg assault, but now at the commotion behind them they turned and saw what was happening. More of the spiders were appearing on the battlements. One of them, larger than its companions and with red-tinted hairs, spat an evil looking liquid at Alston. Luckily it fell short and splatted on the stone.

"By the gods! We have to get out of here!"

The Pict war-horns sounded again and a further hail of slung stones and crossbow bolts hissed through the air and clattered on the floor. Simultaneously there came a fresh series of hammerblows from beneath the trapdoor. The edge of an axe-head protruded through.

"It's too high to jump on to the bridge," Gwen shouted. "It'll shatter our legs. We'll have to risk going down on the southern side into the river –"

"What if the south door's been breached?" Bridget asked. "Their archers can pick us off easily from there."

Gwen's answer was a devil-may-care grin.

Now the northern battlements were thick with spiders hauling themselves over and dropping down to the floor. Gwen's grin vanished as she ran for the south wall. She jumped between two of the battlements' merlons, turned and lowered herself down so that only her hands were visible, then released her grip and dropped.

The others followed swiftly, Will making sure that Bridget was over before he sheathed his sword, turned and lowered himself –

One of the spiders jumped up between his gripping hands, its chitinous legs scrabbling.

Will let go, his last thought before he hit the water being that the world might be enchanted, but it could also be a demon-haunted hell!

*

A long moment later all thoughts
exploded from his brain as he hit the
freezing river. His eyes were closed but he
noted how light became darkness as his
body plunged to the depths. The shock was
like being hit by a bull! Realising his danger,
he got himself moving, kicking with his
legs, paddling his arms as powerfully as he
could to regain the surface. The world above
was a swirling chaos of splintering sunlight
and rippling blue sky. Then his head broke
clear and he drew in the sweetest breath of
his life.

But Will's troubles were not over. His
sodden clothes and the weight of Rowenna's
sword were threatening to drag him under
once more. The dilemma of not wanting to

discard the sword but realising the danger it presented tore at his mind. His head dipped under and Will swallowed a great gulp of muddy water before rising to the surface again.

He began to unbuckle his belt when a muffled voice called to him through the roar of the river –

"Will, over here!" Then, louder. "Will, behind you. Watch out for the hull!"

But he was too slow and too numbed with cold to react. The river swept him against

the boat, his shoulder agonisingly striking wood as the swift current scraped him along the hull towards the vessel's rear. Weakly, hopelessly, Will tried to control his body, to fight against the flow. But his energy had gone and with it any hope that he could save himself. A warm languor crept through him and a luminescence that was no earthly light filled his vision.

Perhaps this is the gateway to the afterlife. I'm going to meet the gods!

Dimly Will was aware of a commotion above him, the clattering of boots on boards. Something snatched at his hair, pulling at it painfully, then his shoulders were gripped by powerful hands and he was hauled upwards.

Well there's no need for Thunor to treat me quite so roughly!

"He's not worth the bother. Should've let him drown."

It was Osbert's voice. Will wondered if *he* had died too, but then he was dropped unceremoniously face down, his nostrils filling with the smell of damp wood. His thoughts began to gather themselves. Gratitude came first, that he had been rescued, then his body started to shake uncontrollably with the biting cold and the shock.

"Someone get a blanket. Puck, turn him over please and check on him."

The voice was sweet but commanding. Will felt the Fool's strong hands turning his unresisting body. Sunlight flooded over him. Puck's blurred face loomed above, blocking the sun, as the jester examined him with professional efficiency.

"Seems he'll live, Princess…"

The blanket came and was draped over him and Will's shudderings began to subside. Another face appeared and dazzled him with a smile.

"P-Princess, it's lovely to see you."

And suddenly he felt alive again and overjoyed to be back in this wonderful world —

Then he heaved, turned on his side and was violently sick.

Chapter 12: Forest Encounters.

A quietness settled over the boat once it was safely underway. The river was fast flowing and the square white sail was stiffened by a favourable wind, so while some vargs kept pace on the west bank for a while, the Picts soon dropped back. Will wondered if they would send runners to the main force still on their journey to the capital.

At Rowenna's bidding Bridget brought round a large jug of mead, from which everybody drank. Will had tasted the sickly sweet liquor a few times before, but as the honeywine burned down his throat and into his stomach he realised it had been brewed to a much higher strength than he was used to, and to his embarrassment he could not suppress a choking cough. Osbert laughed and as if to taunt him further took a huge swig, showed no sign of coughing, and wiped his grinning chops with the back of his hand. Lastly Rowenna drank, made a face and gave a delicate cough herself. Osbert's grin melted away.

With bodies warmed and nerves relaxed by the mead, all the passengers save the tillerman and the lookouts sat together to talk. The first comment came from Bridget, who wondered what were the horrible creatures that could climb sheer walls and squirt poison.

"Spiders obviously," Osbert growled. Puck shook his head.

"I have read of them before but never seen any. They are rare. Also –" he held up a teacherly finger – "they are not entirely of this mortal realm. My parchments are unclear on this, but many sages seem to think that they are forged by enchantments and as such they persist through time. They are not created by god-magic but by some dark human influence, maybe druid. And they are not spiders, strictly speaking, but attercopes, 'poison heads', though I've also seen them called spinners. Some of you may have noticed strands of web as we fought on the tower top."

"I got some of the filth stuck on me," Alston said, showing burn-like marks on the back of one hand and the palm of the other. "It hurts as bad as firesalts."

On seeing this Puck delved into a bag at his belt and took out a small bottle made of dark green glass. "Spread the balm on thickly," he advised, "and it will soothe the pain."

"So will they plague us again?" Rowenna wanted to know. At this the jester could only shrug.

"I said that they persist through time, but the force of magic is like the weather, though in this case it is linked to human upheavals. In times of crisis and war when fear and hatred taint the souls of men the energy that drives any sorcery is stronger and more easily woven by spellcraft —"

Puck broke off suddenly and smiled, realising that he was now delivering a lecture. He made a small bow of apology to the Princess.

"Yes they may plague us again."

The conversation continued for a little while longer, but everyone was tired and soon Rowenna suggested that they get some rest. She moved aft to a sleeping place that had been prepared for her while the others settled where they were, Will and Bridget sharing a blanket, for the afternoon was advancing and the wind cutting across the river was chilled by its waters.

*

Brant moored the boat then reached to hold Rowenna's hand and help her out onto the creaking jetty. Wyatt scrambled to join her, taking a moment to adjust his cleric's habit and put on an imperious face. And then with the Princess in the lead they walked towards what looked to be the not-so-welcoming committee of two men and three women who were waiting on the shore.

One of the men stepped forward. He was lean to the point of being bony and had angular birdlike features.

Like his companions his clothes were
simple; a tunic and breeches made of thick
linen dyed in the tans and greens that would
offer excellent camouflage among the trees.
Also like the others he wore very little
jewellery, just a plain steel ring that may

have been a wedding band or a mark of authority.

"Greetings," he said, though there was no warmth in the word. "I am Wurt, Speaker for the Forester Council." He made a small bow (rather reluctantly Will thought as he watched from the boat).

Rowenna acknowledged the show of etiquette with a slight nod, though her expression was one of sadness as she looked around at the Pict weapons scattered on the ground, having noticed the absence of barges at the jetty.

"You've been attacked…"

"Aye Princess, in the morning twilight two days ago. Pict savages. We had no warning and though we gave a good account of ourselves –" Wurt indicated piles of clothes and weapons that were all that remained of the slain enemy – "they stole our barges and made off downriver."

"That is bad news," Osbert broke in. He looked seriously at the Princess. "They will arrive at Yeavering all the sooner."

"Then we must not be long. Wurt, I would ask you for weapons. And a hot meal would be welcome – your kindness would be appreciated."

It sounded like a request but the Foresters, although a fiercely independent people, were still King Godric's subjects. Everyone present knew how foolish it would be for Wurt to refuse.

His voice became brisk. "I will ask my master shipwright to check the worthiness of your vessels and my men will deliver all the weapons that we can spare. As for food –" He spread his arms wide. "The forest is rich. We will prepare a meal in the food hall. Eat all you please and take with you whatever is left."

"My thanks Wurt, and to your fellow Councillors and your people."

Wurt turned and led the way among the trees. Osbert stayed on the shore to see people off the boat, though when it came to Bridget and Will he put out an arm to stop them.

"Not you two."

"But I'm hungry." Bridget gave the big man a cheeky elfin smile.

"I'll have food brought. You help the shipwright check the boats, and when the weapons arrive stow them neatly and safely. And if you spot anyone or any... thing approaching from upstream, get a move on and warn me quickly."

Will had to admit that these were sensible instructions. He nodded and Osbert stomped off along the path.

The master shipwright turned out to be a woman of around forty years who introduced herself as Nelda. She was strongly built and capable-looking and wore a leather toolbelt around her waist. Like the men she was dressed in linen breeches and tunic, with stout boots to her knees and metal forearm protectors.

"Molten tar burns," she said simply as she saw Will staring. Then she busied herself looking over the hull of the nearer boat, inside and out.

The weapons came before the food and the food, when it did arrive, consisted of a half dozen strips of dried, overcooked venison and two wrinkled apples. When she saw this Nelda laughed, her face lighting up.

"That Osbert, do you annoy him perhaps?"

"He doesn't like us at all." Bridget shrugged as though it was of no importance to her. Nelda made a sympathetic tutting sound and shook her head. She reached into one of the many pouches on her toolbelt and took out what Will saw was a carved wooden disc. She handed it to him.

"When you've finished with the weapons, go to the feast hall and show this to Wurt or one of the other Councillors. It is an estimer, a token of esteem. It shows I am pleased with you. Wurt will explain this to your Princess and then, I'm sure, she will let you feed properly. I don't like bullies either," she added. "I'll stay with the boat until you all return."

Will and Bridget offered their sincere thanks and got on with their task with redoubled enthusiasm.

*

The smoking charcoal pits radiating their heat and the muted chatter of the gathering gave the feast hall a homely feel. And this time the venison was juicy and hot. Will ate with relish. He and Bridget had joined a group that included Brant, Rowenna, two of the Councillors and a clutch of scruffy Forester children. The talk had been of the Pict attack on the community and what the future might hold, but this had not tainted Will's cosy mood until Puck appeared in the doorway and sat down next to him. Briefly Will wondered again why the Fool should be favouring him so.

"It's too quiet out there," Puck said softly. "No night birds calling, no scurryings of animals in the undergrowth. Although I did see something, a silhouette against the clouds. It was a falcon I think."

"Birds roost at night," Brant said dismissively. Puck replied with a tolerant smile and a small shake of the head.

"Older falcons especially are active in the dark." The smile dropped away and the jester shot a sharp glance at Donal, who was bound hand and foot. The Pict boy was still not trusted and for Rowenna's safety Osbert was taking no chances.

"I have heard that druids can see through beasts' eyes. Is that true boy?"

Donal stared at Puck sullenly but didn't answer. His heart was still heavy with the fact that his sister had not been seen since the attack on the river tower, though Bridget had tried to reassure him, pointing out that the group had scattered: not everyone had made it to the boat, but those that didn't might still be alive.

Puck sighed gently, understanding the child's pain. He turned to Will.

"Whether they do or not, if druids can control wild creatures they would surely *increase* their night noises to cover the sound of an approach." He tapped his nose. "This tells me that something is wrong." Then after a pause he added. "Come with me lad and let's check."

Will obeyed at once. He picked up the Forester spear he'd been given to replace the one lost at the tower and followed Puck out of the hall and away from the clearing. The sounds of gentle talking faded to be replaced by cold night air, darkness and the somehow ominous green smell of the vast forest.

The Fool's vague shadow was just a pace in front, his footsteps a soft padding on damp fallen leaves. Will kept close, but his thoughts were elsewhere…

A strange thing was happening. Ordinarily he would have little or no idea of where the Forester settlement was located, for the paths had been winding. But now he could *feel* the direction in which it lay – over his left shoulder. It was as though he was steel being pulled by a lodestone. And there was something else, a looming certainty…

"I think I'm growing your nose," Will said. Puck stopped and suddenly the night was filled with tension. "Don't you sense it t
—"

Then a horn blasted out from the forest before being cut off mid-note.

Chapter 13: Dead Men Standing.

Will and Puck hurried back the way they had come. At one point the jester slowed, unsure of the way, but Will's strange knowledge was unerring. He tugged at Puck's sleeve.

"To the left – I just know it!"

"Maybe you do have my nose, boy – I just hope it isn't the same shape!"

Now it was Will who led and within a few minutes they heard the echoing shouts of orders being given and, shortly afterwards, the light from the campfires in the village clearing. The flames were strong and high and as Will and Puck emerged from the trees they saw men stoking the fires with more dried wood. The brighter glow flung the dark farther from the settlement, but the Foresters and Rowenna's party were wisely taking cover on the shadowed sides of buildings. Entering the village, Will and Puck did the same, joining Osbert, Bragg and four Shields who had formed up into a protective half circle around Rowenna and Wyatt, whose backs were pressed against the dwelling.

"Something's out there," Osbert said, and this time his voice held a rare note of fear.

"Aye. My nose tells me," Puck answered. "But this time because of the stink."

There was indeed a stench of decay in the air that cut through the smell of the woodsmoke. Will thought that it was unholy, a miasma. Something evil. And it was growing stronger to match the growing tightness in Will's chest.

"Whatever it is," he said, "it's coming for us now."

"By the gods!" Bragg pointed a quivering finger.

Beyond the firelight the dark of the night was deepening. The group watched disbelievingly as a wall of blackness slowly advanced, engulfing the trees and, now, the fringes of the village and then the outermost buildings, swallowing them up. And yet the mist-like dark was keeping its shape, folding back on itself on the edges of the open spaces.

"This stuff is being controlled," Puck observed. "Nothing natural behaves like that."

"More druid work?" Rowenna wondered.

"I've not heard of this, but perhaps."

Now the mist bulged, putting out a lobe that touched a campfire and swarmed over it and withdrew, leaving the firewood flameless and cold.

"If all the light goes we'll have no chance," Osbert growled. "But how do we fight fog?"

Will answered him. "It's what's *in* the fog that we must defeat."

It was as though his words were a signal as, nearby, Alston and the twins fired arrows into the blackness – but to no effect for, as soon as the shafts touched it they seemed to slow, then drop harmlessly to the ground.

"We should get back to the boats," Wyatt advised. This provoked an angry response from Osbert.

"Coward! I'm not running from a bit of mist."

"Besides," Rowenna pointed out, "we can't leave the Foresters to fight alone."

"At least we could get you safely away, Princess," Puck said but, at the look she gave him, the jester smiled and let the matter drop.

"I think it's too late anyway," Will said. The others gazed ahead but seemed puzzled. He frowned. "Can't you see them?"

Will had no doubt at what his eyes were showing him; vague white forms moving just inside the wall of darkness. Human in shape but – not – quite…

Then his breath caught as Gwen and Wyatt broke cover and ran at the roiling mass of fog, Wyatt thrusting his spear into its depths. The mist reacted at once, shooting out a tendril that spiralled around the spear shaft and swarmed over Wyatt's hand. He let out a shriek of agony, dropped the spear and staggered back. Gwen moved hurriedly away also, helping Wyatt back to the main group as he nursed his injured hand.

"It's cold, but it burns like fire," he told the others.

Simultaneously other screams sounded from elsewhere in the village as Will saw one of the white shapes flash between two huts and was gone. Then he glimpsed another one out of the corner of his eye, moving at unnatural speed. The main attack was beginning.

Wurt must have realised this too, for he snapped out a strident command that sent his people either running into the forest or taking up strategic positions in the village with bowmen at the vanguard. The Foresters boasted the finest archers in Bernicia, but Will was filled with misgiving at the thought of what had happened to Alston's arrow and those of the twins.

Then the full horror was revealed as a man, or what had once been a man, surged out of the fog bank towards the nearest group. The thing was corpse-white and misshapen, its flesh scabbed and lacerated in places, strings of lank black hair hanging down over its face. And that face was hideous. The eyes were milky white and half hooded by lids of dead skin. The face itself was skeletal, the thing's lips wormlike and black. The grin they made was one of pure malice.

All of this Will absorbed in a second. He heard shocked gasps from the others and, by his side, Bridget gave a soft groan of revulsion.

Three of the Forester archers fired at the thing but because of its speed two missed and the third bounced off the metal boss of the buckler shield it was carrying. The archers made to nock more arrows in their bows, but the corpse was upon them, slaying two within a moment, their bodies crumbling to swirling black clouds of ash. The third archer, a woman, dropped her bow, drew her seax and snatched up a stout log. The creature had started to move towards a huddled group of children. The woman flung herself in its path and slashed at it desperately with cudgel and blade, yelling in dismay as the creature easily fended off her blows.

Then Rowenna, despite Wyatt's yell of alarm, ran forward and thrust her seax deep into the monster's back. It whirled round unharmed and its appalling grin broadened.

Will pushed past Osbert and with all his strength drove his spear right through the body of the thing.

It had no effect. Instead and as though enraged the creature swept its arm round and smashed the buckler into Will's shoulder. Will spun and crashed into a hut wall. But now the Shields were upon the corpse, hacking at it with their swords. Incredibly, disgustingly, even when both arms had been severed the dead man still stood and still advanced until, with one leg cut away, it fell and was quickly chopped to pieces, and only then did it cease moving.

To Will's astonishment, the corpse's flesh remained and did not swirl away as ash. It was as though even the gods would not welcome this abomination into the world beyond the veil.

"More of them!" A shout rang out from someone off to the left. Rowenna and the others looked round, except for Will who happened to see one of the skirmishers kick a limb into the fire close by. The arm hissed briefly in the flames then burst into a cloud of bright yellow sparks, disintegrating. It reminded Will of the flaredust that he'd once seen used at the Festival of Mother's Night years before. His heart lifted.

"Use fire!" he yelled. "Fire will destroy them!"

To spur the people on Will broke cover once again. He grabbed a burning log from one of the fires and dashed towards a lone corpse that Shields had driven away from a cluster of its fellows. He ran round them and jabbed the torch into the thing's face, which immediately caught light although, before its eyes were consumed, it smashed its buckler shield into Will's right side. Will was hurled to the ground but despite the agony from what might have been at least one cracked rib, he grinned in satisfaction at seeing the creature blaze up into a pillar of fire and sparks.

Behind him came cheers and roars. Suddenly people were swarming around, taking up firebrands of their own. Will attempted to stand but the searing pain meant he could only manage to kneel. He saw that the straw roof of one of the dwellings was ablaze, and that Foresters and Shields, fighting together, were driving several of the corpse-things towards it. He was also aware of women taking children by the hand and leading them hurriedly away.

But he felt that all the fight had gone out of him now. Besides, his injury meant that he probably wouldn't stand a chance even if he tried to engage with the enemy. He was very grateful therefore when he saw Bridget running towards him. She had a seax in one hand and a torch in the other. But she was not smiling – her face was taut and grim. She ran past Will and, as he turned painfully, saw her touch the firebrand to the hair of a cadaver, then jab the burning branch into its face. It burst into flame –

But two others nearby turned towards Bridget and Will and stared directly at them.

Chapter 14: Reaper.

Despite his pain and rising terror, Will's mind snatched at the insight – he would call them 'the risen' because someone or something had reanimated them and was *controlling* them now. And while he had discovered their weakness of fire, the real challenge would be to find and somehow destroy the 'reaper' – the thing that had brought them to pseudo-life.

Not that he had time to ponder on it now. The two corpses had started towards him and Bridget who, sensibly, tried to haul Will to his feet rather than tackling the opponents. With Bridget's help Will scrambled up, wincing at the jabbing pain in his side.

"I don't think I can fight," he protested. The look on Bridget's face said, 'You have to!'

So together they stood ready as the risen, eerily silent, broke into a run, bucklers held ready, seaxes raised.

Then there came a warning shout from behind – "Get down!"

Immediately they dropped to a crouch as a clutch of arrows hissed close overhead and lodged themselves in the corpses, briefly bringing them to a halt. This gave Will and Bridget time to stand and hurry – Will was not up to running full speed – towards a blazing bonfire a dozen paces away. They saw that Rowenna's Shields and the Forester bowmen had organised themselves very efficiently, working as fighting units to harry the corpses with arrows and blades, then suddenly creating a space through which one or more torch bearers dashed, touching their firebrands to clothes and hair. In most cases the flames took and quickly afterwards the dried, mummified flesh started to burn. Fallen charred and smoking bodies of reanimated dead lay scattered across the village. Will saw that their number was considerably reduced. This cheered him, together with the fact that many of the Forester people including all of the children had taken to the trees, except where the black wall of roiling fog still lingered in one area.

With Shields and archers nearby and armed now with a firebrand, Will's spirits lifted. He also noted that the pain in his side had become a dull throbbing ache rather than the grating agony of a cracked or broken bone. The next few minutes were going to hurt, but at least he would be able to play his part as necessary.

The bowmen loosed another round of arrows and Shields in crescent formation moved in, hacking at the risen then, at a shouted command, breaking the line so that Bridget and Will could move in. With a sudden surge of anger and disgust Will jammed the torch into the corpse's mouth before sweeping it across the thing's filthy rags and straggling hair. It caught light immediately, though its sightless eyes seemed to burn with an equal heat until they were consumed by the flames and the cadaver collapsed like a pile of dropped sticks.

With no enemy in the immediate vicinity now, Will had time to survey the scene. Groups of Shields were moving in lockstep, driving corpses towards campfires that other men kept well alight, or into range of archers or torch bearers. He also caught sight of Puck fighting with the skill of a battle-honed warrior and Brant and Osbert standing with Rowenna, who was also wielding a sword skilfully and gaining ground against the foe.

Will reflected that for all his dislike of Osbert, he was fiercely loyal to his Princess and would undoubtedly die for her. Will's resentment of the man dropped a notch.

A veil of bluegrey smoke from the fires and burning bodies drifted across the battlefield. As it cleared, Will was puzzled to see that lines of it remained. *Lines?* He looked again more closely, checking himself. No, his first impression had been right. Not only that, but the wavering smokelike threads were mysteriously attached at one end to the skulls of the risen, reaching back across the clearing before they disappeared into a narrow alley between two of the settlement's larger buildings.

Will shook Bridget's arm and pointed out the spidery lines, frowning then at her puzzled expression.

"You don't see them?"

"*I* don't," she said, making Will smile at the absence of doubt in her voice.

Then they rejoined the fray, though when they stepped in to set light to two more cadavers, Will dodged round and passed his hand through the smokeline of one of them. And, just as with ordinary smoke, his hand met no resistance – but the thread did not dissipate. Not only that, he also felt a definite *presence* within it, a controlling force wielding its influence through the filament. On an impulse he wafted his firebrand through it, to no effect. Then he set the creature's clothes alight and stepped back, dragging Bridget with him.

"I know what's going on," he said excitedly, giving Bridget a quick explanation. He pointed along the weave of threads that only he could see.

"He – it – is over there, between those buildings."

"So –"

"So the Shields and Foresters have more or less got the upper hand here. I say we attack the source, if we can."

Bridget frowned then shrugged, miming a quick lunge and parry before giving a smile and a nod.

"Right behind you partner."

They circled around the outer ring of huts to reach the buildings from the other side. Will gestured for Bridget to stay put, while he crouched low to peer round into the ally.

Smoke blurred the scene somewhat, mixed as it was with the same writhing fog that had brought the corpses. But silhouetted clearly enough against the fireglow coming from the clearing was a human figure, the figure of a tall woman with her back to them.

She wore flowing black robes and her equally dark hair waved and billowed around her.

The woman's arms were outstretched
and from her black-gloved hands emanated
the smokelines that gave her power over the
corpses, one of which stood guard close

beside her, a huge figure in the flickering light.

At Will's bidding Bridget craned to look round, but then shook her head, seeing nothing but the solitary cadaver.

"If she's mortal we can kill her," Will whispered. "I saw a dropped bow and quiver of arrows back there – and do you have a throwing knife?"

"I do. But how skilled are you –"

"I was thinking you might do it – just aim for the darkest patch of smoke. If you can wound her she'll turn to answer the attack. Then I can put an arrow in her eye."

So saying, Will hurried to retrieve the bow. He nocked an arrow and pulled back the bowstring, nodding to Bridget. The girl stepped out from behind the building and, with a doubtful sigh, threw the knife –

Will saw it fly fast and true, end over end, sinking into the reaper's thigh. The woman made a sound halfway between a scream and a snarl. Her arms dropped and the guard collapsed. Simultaneously ragged cheering sounded from the battlefield as the other risen fell to the ground.

Will stepped forward and as the reaper turned, he loosed the arrow. And his aim would have been true if she had not moved. Instead she twisted aside and as the arrow whizzed past, she leaned round and drew the blade from her leg. Then she made some rune-like pattern in the air, bringing dark tendrils back into being. One of them snaked to the fallen guard who juddered, rose –

And came charging towards Bridget and Will.

Chapter 15: Flight.

Bridget muttered some hurried words that sounded like an invocation to the gods. Will fitted another arrow to his bow, aimed and fired – not at the corpse but at the reaper. The tip pierced her right shoulder. Again came the unearthly snarling scream and again the smokeline faded so that the cadaver crashed to the ground. The woman staggered back under the arrow's impact into the firelit clearing.

Looking beyond her, Will saw that with the corpses downed, both Foresters and Angalsax stood by indecisively. Osbert, Puck, Brant, Bragg and Gwen formed a protective circle around Rowenna. The Princess was talking quickly to her Champion, gesturing to various parts of the clearing. But whatever she intended didn't happen, for now the reaper, with Will's arrow still protruding from her shoulder, flung her arms wide and sent a spray of smokelines radiating into the night.

Immediately Will drew his seax and moved towards her. As he jumped over the fallen corpse a smokeline quivered past him and a powerful hand gripped his ankle, sending him sprawling. With great presence of mind Bridget leaped forward and drove her seax through the cadaver's hand as Will squirmed round and hacked at the wrist with his blade. Four desperate blows severed the limb. Will kicked it aside and scrabbled upright.

The reaper had moved out of sight, perhaps taking cover between other buildings or maybe among the trees. Wherever she had hidden she was working her dark magic again. Smokelines lashed across the clearing into the swirling fogbank and within a few seconds a score of the risen appeared, scattering quickly as they selected their targets. Will reached the end of the alley. The lines were converging off to his left, and his second guess had been correct; the reaper had taken to the trees where she would be much more difficult to find. He wondered briefly if he should try to locate her or join the fight against the newly arrived risen. But two things swept the problem aside –

Rowenna had clearly issued new orders. Osbert broke from the circle and was instructing the Angalsax to leave. The Foresters had made a similar decision. The bowmen were backing towards the trees, fending off the risen attack with round after round of arrows.

Secondly, Will heard Bridget's warning cry and dodged aside just in time to avoid the cadaver's clawed hand. Will slashed with his seax, distracting the corpse just long enough for Bridget to slip past.

"Everyone's going," Will said. "We must get to the boats."

While many of the corpses were lightning-quick, the risen that had guarded the reaper could manage no more than a shambling lurch. Bridget and Will could easily outpace it. Will's intention had been to join Rowenna's group, both to help protect the Princess and to *seek* protection among some of the Angalsax's finest warriors. He was halfway across the clearing with Bridget at his side when she grabbed his arm and brought him to a stop.

"Donal," she said breathlessly. "Do you think someone untied him?"

Will groaned. He had last seen the Pict boy bound hand and foot in the food hall. But surely even someone as hard hearted as Osbert wouldn't just leave him to die!

Will shook his head, shrugged. Bridget's expression was set.

"We've got to check."

Of course, that's the right thing to do, Will thought, though the first stabs of panic clutched at his heart as he followed her hurrying figure. The battle had tipped to the reaper's advantage with the arrival of more of the risen. Rowenna's command for her soldiers to break off and escape was plain common sense. But no doubt they would be pursued through the forest, and then there was the time it would take to board the boats and cast off…

There would be no question of waiting for any late stragglers.

They reached the food hall and rushed inside. The space was gloomy with only a few torches burning, most of them having been taken to use against the enemy. Bridget called out and at once there came an answering cry from across the room. The boy had squirmed under a table in a desperate bid to avoid being seen.

While Will kept watch at the doorway, Bridget ran across and cut Donal's bonds. Then they both joined Will and together they began to hurry towards the forest path that led to the river. But because the Angalsax had taken that route, the risen were congregating there aiming to follow.

"We'll have to avoid it and push through the undergrowth," Will said. They veered away, hoping that none of the corpses would see them.

Once they had crossed the treeline, they paused briefly to get their breath. As Will's racing heartbeat slowed and his mind settled, he became aware once again of the living land around him – the *sense* of where things were. Obviously the village was behind him, but in his mind's eye he could see various paths radiating away like faint blue ribbons into the forest depths and felt the pull of the river, again like lodestone to steel, ahead and to the right.

Wordlessly he set off, Bridget and Donal keeping close for the darkness was intense.

At times, the going was easy; the group could tramp through clumps of ferns and dogwood with little effort. Holly and bramble could be avoided, but screens of leatherwyrt needed to be tackled by brute force, hacked down with seaxes, adding precious minutes to the journey time.

But at last they heard the soft roar of the river and shortly afterwards men's voices. With renewed effort they broke through to the sloping bank of the shoreline and saw the flicker of torches off to the left at the jetty.

As they drew closer Will called and Brant hailed back. He was standing on the gunwale of one boat with a foot planted on the jetty to keep the vessel steady. Will could make out the other boat mid-water, with Rowenna steering.

"Hurry now," Brant urged.

Will, Bridget and Donal reached the jetty, Will indicating for the others to go first. As he started to follow some instinct made him turn round. Fear surged through him as a wall of black fog swirled out of the trees and engulfed him before he could move. He shrieked at the freezing touch of it and at the feeling that the very life force was being sucked out of him.

He flung himself backwards and slammed down onto the jetty, then desperately rolled and pushed himself upright. To his horror he saw that Brant, terrified by what was happening, had slipped the mooring line from its post and was using an oar to push the boat out into the water. At once the current began to take it downstream.

The three of them, Will, Bridget and Donal ran desperately along the jetty. Bridget leapt first and managed to grab the gunwale. Brant dragged her aboard. Ignoring the waves of pain from his bruised ribcage, Will broke into a run and made a massive leap. It was not enough. He hit the gunwale on his stomach, driving the air from his lungs in a gush and, badly stunned, slid off into the water. Donal had no chance of making the jump. He dove into the river and with a few swift strokes swam to Will and supported him as he got his breath back.

"Thanks," Will gasped at last. He turned himself around to locate the boat. It was maybe ten yards away. The rowers had shipped their oars to give Will and Donal chance to catch up, but the current was bearing the vessel steadily downriver.

Then Will looked towards the jetty. The tide of black fog had reached the waterline and now it disgorged at least six of the risen who, without hesitation, jumped into the water and came wading towards them.

Chapter 16: Yeavering.

Wading – not swimming.

"I don't think they can swim, Donal," Will said. "Come on, we've got to move."

The leading corpse was just a couple of yards from Donal's frantically kicking legs. Will knew that there was nothing he could do to protect the boy. He still had his seax but the strength of his blows would be greatly reduced by the water, and the throbbing pain in his chest was intense. But Donal wasn't panicking. He understood the situation, oriented his body towards the boat and began to swim in a more controlled manner. Yet the corpses were still advancing, up to their shoulders now in the water. Will saw their control lines arching above them towards the fogbank on the shore, which was moving slowly, keeping pace.

Now Donal had come up level with Will and swam past him. The nearest corpse was an armspan away. Perhaps losing its footing, it dipped below the surface and the smokeline became detached. A moment later the creature re-emerged and the thread reattached itself.

But that gave Will an idea. He began sweeping water over the cadaver's head, causing the thread to break contact again and again. The action was also moving him into deeper water. Finally, the creature submerged and did not reappear. The smokeline quivered for a moment and then faded. The other risen, unable to go out of their depth, turned and moved back slowly towards the shore.

Fire and water, Will thought jubilantly. *Essential to humans, deadly to risen!*

*

After they had been travelling for several hours, Rowenna ordered the boats to put-in on the western bank. The rowers were exhausted and gratefully obeyed.

"The reaper will probably still be coming after us, Princess," Osbert advised. Rowenna nodded.

"I'm aware of it. But we are all cold, hungry and tired. Have some campfires made up and post lookouts so that we'll have fair warning if any risen appear. We won't stay long."

Once the fires were lit and the food passed round, Rowenna asked the others in the group what they knew about necromancy – reaper-craft. No one had much to say, not even Puck whose knowledge of occult lore was extensive.

"Like attercopes, reapers are uncommon." He shrugged. "It is said that they suck the souls from dying humans who have no god-mark over their heart. Then they use that energy to reanimate the dead."

Will added, "I have read that like vargs, reapers exist only partly in this world and partly in the netherworld. Because of that, their power waxes and wanes as the veil between the realms changes."

Puck nodded. "I believe that is so. The fact that we are now seeing reapers, spinners *and* vargs is a very dark omen."

"Also…" Will went on to explain that while he and Donal were struggling in the water, he had glimpsed the reaper riding what seemed to be a black horse-like creature, apparently made from the same substance as the fog itself. "Perhaps the reaper too is created by the fog."

"Did anyone else see it?" Osbert asked almost aggressively. There was a shaking of heads. "Then what makes you so special, nithing?"

Will didn't have the energy to answer even though he was heartily sick of the man's sniping and insults. But when Puck put his hand on his shoulder, a gesture of camaraderie, his spirits lifted.

Later, as the fires were being put out and people began stowing provisions, Puck took Will aside. "You must be wary," the Fool said. "Osbert hasn't thought on this deeply and I don't think anyone else has, but because you can see reapers and the threads that control the risen, somebody might get it into their heads that *you* are somehow connected with the dark arts. And if that suspicion spreads…"

Puck left the rest unsaid, but Will knew it meant that he would probably have Woden's god-mark cut from him and then most likely be executed.

"Then I should –"

"As your powers develop, confide only in those you trust absolutely."

It was only later that he realised the import of what the jester had said.

*

They had put to shore two miles north of Yeavering's docks as a precaution, not knowing if the Picts had already arrived – two hundred of them, and perhaps more if the ones who had stolen the horses had joined them. *And*, Will thought with a sigh, *maybe druids and vargs – oh yes, and the reaper and her gang of corpses!* He had a brief but glorious image of the risen fighting with the Picts and vargs, destroying them before he gallantly moved in to finish off the reaper and end the entire threat –

The vision faded to be replaced by one that was more likely, of Pict forces assembled in the forest waiting for their moment to strike. And that picture remained in Will's mind as whatever wasn't needed for the final leg of the journey was stowed away on the boats. Osbert had warned everyone earlier that they would now need to travel on foot, since approaching the capital from the river would render them far too vulnerable to Pict crossbow and sling fire.

"At least when we break clear of the forest, we can form up the Shield Wall to maximise our chances of getting inside Yeavering's walls."

As the party moved off a gentle drizzle began to fall from the lead-grey sky. A stiffening wind sent low clouds streaming across. The drizzle soon chilled them, but at least it damped down the fallen leaves so that the travellers' passage through the trees was silent save for the occasional snapping of a twig.

And all the while everyone was on constant alert for the enemy. Once, Will fancied he heard distant voices but he immediately doubted that, thinking his imagination was plaguing him again. There was only the quiet hush of the breeze through the leaf canopy and the gentle hiss of the rain. And the rapid thumping of his own heart.

After about an hour Osbert held up a hand to bring the group to a halt. Not far ahead of them lay the vast clearing around the capital. From where he was standing Will could see no Picts out there, no sign of battle. That might mean they had not yet arrived, which was the general feeling or, more worryingly, that they were hiding in the forest ready to ambush.

Osbert turned to face the group. "Once we're out in the open we'll form up around the Princess. He glared at Bridget and Will. "Hopefully you will not prove to be totally worthless and fight anyone or anything that tries to prevent the Princess from getting inside the gates. I've got us this far – don't mess up the last bit."

Again Will was not minded to reply. He shrugged, wondering what the survival chances would be for himself, Bridget and the few others who were not to be part of the shield.

Rowenna stepped forward a little in front of Osbert and addressed her people, the brave little band that had brought her this far. Her voice was calm and the tone was quietly determined.

"Thank you all for the outstanding bravery you've shown. We're almost home and, once there, *we'll* become the hunters."

They moved off cautiously. The drizzle had almost stopped. Clouds were thinning and the first light of dawn was showing in the east. Some way off from the treeline, Puck bade the others stop while he scouted ahead. A few minutes later he returned, his face unreadable. He spoke quietly to Osbert and Rowenna. They listened intently to him and then Rowenna walked quickly to the edge of the forest, the others gathering behind.

The morning light was strengthening and the world was cast in greys.

Will heard the Princess's breath catch in her throat.

"That's impossible," she whispered.

Then Rowenna, smart, confident, battle-trained Princess of Bernicia, sank to her knees in despair.

*

The story continues in Battle Book 2:

United We Stand

United We Stand

(Coming in 2021)

Savage Pict tribes rampage through the Angalsax kingdom of Bernicia and soul-sucking reapers follow with their walking-dead soldiers destroying all before them.   Will Foundling, orphan outsider, military scholar and would-be warrior, must find a way to help his beloved princess rally her people. Bridget, a sassy battle-runner with hidden talents, helps him stand against hatred and prejudice on all sides but how will she react to Will's growing ability in a forbidden magic?

With only a rag-tag collection of other outsiders firmly on their side, can Will and Bridget unite friends and foes to survive the dark devastation sweeping down from the north?

United We Stand is the second in a series of novels where Will and his allies and rivals gradually discover the secrets behind the kingdom's invasion and Will's terrifying birthright whilst battling to help save not just their own people, but all of humankind.

The Battle Project

Divided we fall is part of a planned series of action-packed books and games based in the alternative, darkly magical Anglo-Saxon world initially dreamed up by Gareth Mottram. Although the project could lead anywhere, works published or in development at the moment include:

Published
- **Divided We Fall** by Gareth Mottram   (Book/ebook)
- **Divided We Fall - For Younger Readers** by Steve Bowkett (Book/ebook)

In Development
- **United We Stand** by Gareth Mottram (Book/ebook - to be published early 2021)
- **United We Stand – For Younger Readers** by Steve Bowkett (Book/ebook)
- **Battle: Word Warriors** by Steve Bowkett with additional material by Gareth Mottram (educational book)
- **Battle: The Card Game** by Gareth Mottram (strategic card and board game)

 You can read the latest updates on all of these projects on: www.facebook.com/battle.novels

Steve Bowkett: Author

I was born and brought up in the mining valleys of South Wales and started writing for pleasure at the age of thirteen shortly after moving to the Leicester area, where I still live.

My background is in education. I taught English for 20 years in Leicestershire High Schools, though I'm now a full-time writer, storyteller, educational consultant and also a qualified hypnotherapist.

I have written fantasy and SF for teenagers, adult and teen horror, romance, mainstream fiction for pre-teens, fiction and non-fiction for younger readers and poetry for all ages. I have also brought out a number of educational books, principally in the fields of literacy, creativity, thinking skills and emotional resourcefulness. To date I have published 79 titles plus numerous short stories and poems.

Find out more at: www.stevebowkett.co.uk

Tony Hitchman: Artist

As a a boy Tony Hitchman used to spend all his time reading comics, drawing cartoons and watching films. Now he's an adult (allegedly) he spends his time reading comics, drawing cartoons and watching films.

Tony has written scripts for the comic publisher DC Thompson, contributed cartoons and comic strips to various small press publications, illustrated educational books and collaborated with Steve Bowkett on two books for teachers "Using Comic Art to Improve Speaking, Reading and Writing" and "Developing Thinking Skills through Creative Writing."

Printed in Poland
by Amazon Fulfillment
Poland Sp. z o.o., Wrocław

66619661R00130